Mostly Ghostly

One Night In Doom House

3

Experience all the chills of the Mostly Ghostly series!

Mostly Ghostly 3

One Night In Doom House

R.L. STINE

DELACORTE PRESS
A PARACHUTE PRESS BOOK

Published by
Delacorte Press
an imprint of
Random House Children's Books
a division of Random House, Inc.
New York

Visit us on the Web! www.randomhouse.com/kids
Educators and librarians, for a variety of teaching tools, visit us at
www.randomhouse.com/teachers

Library of Congress Cataloging-in-Publication Data is
available upon request.

ISBN: 0-385-74665-2 (trade)
0-385-90915-2 (lib. bdg.)

Printed in the United States of America

January 2005

10 9 8 7 6 5 4 3 2 1

BVG

i

"**NICKY, REMEMBER THE TIME** we were all having dinner at Scruffy's? And you squeezed the ketchup dispenser and accidentally squirted Dad in the face?"

I grinned at my sister, Tara. "What made you think it was an accident?"

"Because you wouldn't do a thing like that on purpose," Tara said. "You're always such a *good* boy." She pinched my cheek. She knows I hate that.

I shoved her hand away.

"Remember? The waitress saw Dad and screamed. She thought his head was bleeding. She started to call 911."

"Of course I remember," I said. My voice broke. Sometimes it was hard to think about those days.

Tara and I crossed Main Street. Snow was falling in big soft flakes. Our shoes didn't make a sound as we hurried over the snowy sidewalk. I glanced down and saw that we weren't leaving any footprints.

Town was crowded with Saturday afternoon shoppers. But no one noticed Tara and me.

No one noticed us because we are ghosts—which means we are invisible.

Tara tugged her red wool ski cap down over her dark hair. "You know what I hate about being dead?" she asked.

"No. What?"

"Everything," she said.

I didn't answer. What could I say?

Two boys came running out of Sweets 'N' Treats on the corner, carrying big bags of Gummi Worms. One of them ran right into me. He knocked me off my feet, and I stumbled into a parked car.

"Hey, watch where you're going!" Tara shouted.

Of course the boys couldn't hear her. They continued on, boots crunching the snow, slurping red and yellow worms into their mouths one at a time.

Tara scooped some snow into her mittens, made a snowball—and heaved it hard. It made a nice *thwok* as it hit the boy in the back of the neck.

His bag of Gummis went flying into the snow. He spun around. "Who threw that?" he shouted.

Oops. No one there.

I laughed. "See? There are *some* good things about being a ghost."

"It's the pits," Tara muttered. "I tried phoning some of my friends yesterday. They just kept saying, 'Hello? Hello? Hello?' They couldn't hear me. How do you think that made me feel?"

"Bad?"

She shoved me. "Don't make fun of me, Nicky. It isn't funny."

"I know," I said. "But I have a really good feeling about today. I don't know why, but I think we're going to find Mom and Dad."

Last October, as soon as Tara and I realized we were ghosts, we hurried to our house. We expected to find Mom and Dad waiting for us.

But we had a shock in store for us. Another family—the Doyle family—had moved in. Wow. That was a bad moment. To come home and find strangers living in your house!

How creepy is *that*?

Where were our parents? What had happened to us?

Tara and I were bursting with questions. But we couldn't ask them. You see, Mr. and Mrs. Doyle and their older son, Colin, couldn't see or hear us.

But to our surprise, Max Doyle—who is my age, eleven—could see and hear us just fine.

Poor Max was terrified at first. *No way* did he want to be haunted by two ghosts. He didn't have any answers for Tara and me. He didn't have a clue about what happened to us or where our parents went.

Max begged us to leave. He tried to chase us away. But then he saw how frightened Tara and I were. And how sad. And he promised to help us.

Now it was January, and Tara and I were still hunting for our parents.

We were wearing old sweaters and winter parkas that Max had dug up for us. The snowflakes continued to fall, dancing in the wind, as we made our way to Scruffy's Diner at the end of Main Street.

Tara and I had a desperate plan. But I had a really good feeling about it.

I just *knew* we'd find Mom and Dad today.

2

THE SKY DARKENED AS Tara and I stepped up to the little restaurant. Yellow light poured onto the snow from the big front window. We tried to peek in, but the window was totally steamed up.

Scruffy's Diner looks like a train car. It's long and low with a shiny metal front. A sign on the flat roof blinks GOOD EATS on and off in bright blue neon.

As I pulled open the glass front door, we were greeted by the aroma of French fries and hamburgers sizzling on the grill. I took a deep breath. Sweet!

"Wow! It's crowded," Tara said, glancing down the long row of blue and red booths. She slapped her mittens together, trying to warm up her hands.

Just because we're ghosts doesn't mean we don't get cold.

I stomped my boots to get the snow off.

"Look out!" I cried.

Tara and I leaped out of the way as a blue-uniformed waitress hurried past carrying a platter of sandwiches and shakes.

I grabbed the coatrack to catch my balance. It tipped a little and a few coats fell on the floor. I picked them up quickly. I hoped no one saw the coats floating by themselves back onto the hooks.

Tara pointed to the booth in back by the kitchen. "Our old booth—it's empty. Race you!"

We took off, running full speed down the narrow aisle between the booths.

"Whoa!" I slipped in a puddle on the floor and fell into a booth jammed with high school kids. They all cried out in surprise as their hamburgers and fries went sliding off the table.

"Oops. Sorry."

Of course they didn't hear me. They started arguing about who did it. "Maybe it was an earthquake!" a boy said.

A girl called to the waitress. "Miss? Miss? There's something wrong with this table!"

I pulled myself up quickly, wiping coleslaw off my coat, and made my way to our booth. Tara was already sitting down, gazing at the menu.

"Nicky, the menu is exactly the same," she said as I climbed in across from her. "And here we are in our old booth. Nothing has changed. Except . . . Except . . ."

Except Mom and Dad aren't here.

Tara hid her face behind the menu. She didn't want me to see her crying.

She's only nine, but she's very tough. She hardly ever cries.

But being in Scruffy's without Mom and Dad was really hard—for both of us.

You see, our parents took us to Scruffy's every Saturday afternoon. We always loaded up on burgers and fries and Scruffy Shakes—thick shakes with lumps of ice cream in them. Then we'd go to the mall or to the movies.

Every Saturday afternoon.

And we always sat in this booth.

So, this is our big idea. . . . If we sit in this same booth on a Saturday afternoon at the same time we always came here—maybe . . . just *maybe* . . . Mom and Dad will show up.

Of course it's crazy.

Crazy and sad at the same time.

But Tara and I are desperate. It's been four months, and we still don't have a clue about how to find Mom and Dad.

So we'll try *anything.*

Even sitting in this booth and waiting.

"I think I'm really hungry," Tara said.

Ghosts get cold. And they get hungry, too. At least *we* do.

"I don't think the waitress will take our order," I said. "You know. Since she can't see us and can't hear us."

"No problem." Tara slid out of the booth.

Uh-oh.

"Hey, wait!" I called. "Tara—what are you *doing*? Tara—wait!"

But it was a waste of breath. You can't stop my sister when she wants to do something.

I watched her trot up to the booth with all the high school kids. They were still arguing about who spilled their food. Tara picked up two plates of French fries and started back to our booth with them.

A hush fell over the table. The teenagers stared at the two plates floating in midair. Then they scrambled out of the booth, pulling on their coats and hats.

"Whoa, dude—too weird! I'm outta here!"

"Outta my way!"

Tara and I watched them run out the door as we helped ourselves to the French fries. They were hot and greasy and really salty. Excellent!

But before we could finish, a waitress stepped in front of our table. "This booth is free," she called to a man and woman behind her. "Let me just clear away these French fries."

The waitress grabbed our plates and stepped back to let the man and woman slide into our booth. They both wore jeans and black leather jackets and carried white motorcycle helmets. The man dropped his helmet on the seat next to me.

"Nicky, help me!" Tara screamed. "She's sitting on my lap!"

"What do you expect *me* to do?" I cried. "*Ouch!* He's sitting on me! And he weighs a ton!"

"She's *crushing* me!" Tara wailed.

I couldn't see Tara at all. The woman had her totally covered.

"Tickle her!" I said.

The guy leaned back on me, and I groaned. Pain shot up and down my whole body. He had his dark hair tied in a ponytail, and the ponytail swished back and forth in my eyes.

"I'm tickling her ribs," Tara said. "But she doesn't feel it. Maybe she isn't ticklish."

"Bad news," I groaned. "This big geek is sitting on my hands. I can't even *try* to tickle him."

The man and woman leaned over the table, holding hands.

"What'll it be?" the waitress asked them.

"I'll have the vegetable soup," the woman said.

"I'll have the same," the man said. "And bring a lot of crackers."

"I'm crushed. I'm totally crushed," Tara wailed.

The guy leaned back again, pushing his greasy ponytail into my face. I let out another groan. "Tara—remind me to breathe later."

A few minutes later, the waitress set two large blue bowls of soup on the table. The guy dug his elbow into my chest as he reached for a package of crackers.

I slipped my arms free as he crushed the crackers in his hand and dumped them into his soup. "Tara, what do you think?" I asked. "We pick up the bowls and dump the soup in their laps?"

Tara let out another groan. "Do we have a choice?"

3

TARA AND I PUSHED open the front door of the diner. We could still hear the screams of the man and woman from the booth in the back. We stepped out onto the snow and took deep breaths of the cold fresh air.

Tara pulled down her ski cap and I slid the parka hood over my head. The snowflakes had stopped falling. The wind gusted in our faces. We ducked our heads and started for home.

"What a waste of good vegetable soup," I said.

Tara shook her head sadly. "This was such a bad-news idea. What made us think Mom and Dad would show up at the diner?" Her voice shook.

"It seemed like a good plan," I muttered. An SUV roared past, splashing slush on us.

Tara turned to me. "What if we never find them, Nicky? What if we never see Mom and Dad again?" Her chin trembled. Tears made her dark eyes shimmer.

I slapped her on the back. "We'll find them," I said. "Remember that note we found? It fell out from the back of the framed photo of Mom and Dad? It said we shouldn't worry. That they were really close."

"But if they're so close, *where are they?*" Tara cried.

I didn't know how to answer. I just let out a long sigh.

We'd been searching for Mom and Dad ever since we got home. And we weren't the only ones looking for them. Some evil ghosts were searching for them too.

We *had* to find them before those ghosts did. We had to keep trying new ways. We couldn't give up.

Tara and I stepped into the house. Our old house—143 Bleek Street. But it didn't feel much like home with the Doyle family living in it.

"The Doyles are out," Tara said. "The place is empty."

We started up the stairs to Max's room. But a loud crash from the kitchen made us stop. Tara turned to me, her eyes wide with fear. "Who—?"

We heard someone humming. A woman's voice.

"Lulu!" Tara whispered.

Lulu, our old housekeeper, is a ghost too. She pops up in the kitchen from time to time. We beg her to tell us about Mom and Dad. But she's very old and her spirit is very faint. She tries to help us. She really does. But we haven't learned much from her.

Maybe today . . .

"Glory, glory, it's good to see you kids!" Lulu exclaimed as we hurried into the kitchen. She wore a white apron over her long gray jumper. Her white hair was tied tightly in a bun behind her head.

She bent to pick up a frying pan from the floor. "I . . . I was making breakfast for you. But the pan slipped out of my hands. Glory, how foolish."

I helped Lulu pick up the pan. There were eggs sizzling inside it. We set it on the stove.

"So weak these days," Lulu said, starting to fade from sight. "Glory, I feel so weak. Can't even hold a frying pan. . . ."

She vanished. The kitchen grew silent except for the ghostly eggs sizzling in the pan.

"Lulu, come back!" Tara pleaded. "We need to talk to you. Come back!"

Lulu's spatula appeared, floating by itself in the air. Then her pale arm, skin sagging. Then the rest of her. "Glory, it's good to see you."

"Lulu, help us," Tara said. She grabbed the old woman's hand. "Mom and Dad were scientists, right. And—"

"Such smart people," Lulu interrupted. "Everyone said so."

"And they captured a bunch of evil ghosts and locked them up somewhere, right?" Tara continued. "But a ghost named Phears helped the evil ghosts escape."

"The eggs are burning," Lulu said, scraping the pan with the spatula. "Glory, I feel so weak again."

"*No!*" Tara shouted. She reached out for Lulu's hand. "I won't let you get away. You have to help us."

"Phears and his cat," Lulu said. "That Phears was an evil one. But glory, he loved his cat."

"Where did all those ghosts go?" I asked. "They're our only clue. Maybe they can lead us to Mom and Dad."

"Do you know anything about those ghosts?" Tara demanded.

"Glory," Lulu whispered, and disappeared again.

Somehow the spatula ended up in Tara's hand. The pan of eggs had vanished with Lulu.

We waited without moving. It seemed like hours, but finally Lulu returned, faint now, a blur of gray and white. "Colder than the grave," she whispered. "That's what you will need, children. Colder than the grave."

"Lulu, what does that mean?" I cried. "Please—tell us what that means."

But she was gone again. And this time we knew it was for good.

Tara shook her head hard. "She didn't make any sense, Nicky."

I nodded. "She was trying to tell us something. But . . ." My voice trailed off. I had a heavy feeling in my stomach. Wasn't there *anyone* who could help us?

"Max," Tara muttered. Had she been reading my thoughts? "Where *is* Max? We need his help— desperately."

I thought hard.

"Oh, yeah. You remember," I said finally. "Max and his friend went to some crazy haunted house."

4

AARON PULLED ME UP the twisting walk to the creepy old house. The wind howled, making the scraggly hedges bend and creak. All along the front wall, the gray, stained shingles shook and the window shutters rattled. The whole house appeared to shiver and quake in the blowing wind.

"I really don't want to go in this house," I said through gritted teeth. I brushed snowflakes off my eyebrows. "We're going to freeze our tails off in there, Aaron."

"So?" He stared at me through his swim goggles. Aaron wears swim goggles wherever he goes. I once asked him why. He thought about it a long time, then said he didn't know.

He never wears long pants. He only wears shorts—even on the snowiest days.

Yes, Aaron is totally weird. But he's also my best friend, so what can I do?

"You want to see ghosts, don't you, Max?" Aaron had to shout over the howling wind.

"No. Not really," I replied.

I have plenty of ghosts at home.

That's what I wanted to tell Aaron. I had tried to tell him about Nicky and Tara a few times. But each time, he thought I was joking or making up a story. He refused to believe me.

Yes, I have ghosts back home. I don't need to visit a haunted house to see ghosts.

But here we were, up to our knees in snow on a Saturday night, trudging up to the hulking gray house known as the Grover Mansion.

A haunted house. A *real* one. That's what most people in town believed.

My brother, Colin, told me it took the Grover family thirty years to build the place. That's because it's as big as some castles.

And when it came time for the Grovers to die, they refused to go—because they wanted to stay in the house forever. And so the Grovers haunt the house to this day. And they come out every night just before dawn.

Of course, Colin is a big liar. But everyone in town has a story about the Grover Mansion. Everyone thinks it's haunted.

The house has been abandoned for years. The whole block is deserted. Just overgrown lawns and shabby empty houses with shutters banging and the wind whistling through holes in the roofs.

You can't blame people for moving away. Who wants to live next to a haunted house?

We stepped onto the front stoop. The welcome mat was half covered in snow. I kicked the snow away to read the mat. It didn't say WELCOME. It said GOOD-BYE.

"Check out the mailbox," Aaron said.

I turned and read the name on the rusted mailbox: DOOM HOUSE.

I shivered. Not from fright. From the snow and freezing wind. "Aaron, let's go," I said. "We're not going to see any real ghosts here. And we're going to get in major trouble staying overnight. If our parents find out . . ." I shivered again.

"They're not going to find out," Aaron said. "Your parents think you're at my house. And my parents think I'm at your house."

"But—but—" I sputtered.

"And what if we really see some ghosts?" he said. He raised his camcorder. "What if we see ghosts and we get them on tape? Then we'll be famous. We'll be on TV. We'll be celebrities. And Ms. McDonald will have to let us do our social studies project on ghosts."

"But she said we couldn't do our project on ghosts, remember?" I said. "Ms. McDonald said ghosts aren't social studies. She assigned us a project—remember? The history of Paraguay?"

Aaron made a face. "Paraguay? What's a Paraguay?"

"About three pounds," I said.

Aaron didn't laugh at my joke. "Max, maybe Ms. McDonald will change her mind. If we find real ghosts and get them on the camcorder, she'll *have* to change her mind. And maybe she won't flunk me and make me do fifth grade all over again."

You see, Aaron was in major trouble. He never did any homework. He just didn't believe in it.

But Ms. McDonald finally put her foot down. She said if Aaron didn't get an A on this project, he'd have to repeat fifth grade. And maybe third and fourth grade too!

"Look, Aaron, there aren't going to be any ghosts in here and you know it," I argued. "It's just an old house that's been empty for a lot of years. Someone made up a ghost story about it, and someone else made up another one. And now everyone believes them. But they're just made-up stories."

I shivered again and pulled my parka tighter. I stamped my boots on the GOOD-BYE mat. My feet were both frozen numb.

Aaron grabbed the rusted doorknob. "Come on. If we don't see anything by dawn, we can go. And we'll do a project on the history of ghosts in Paraguay."

"Ha, ha," I said. My lips were frozen too. I could barely open my mouth to laugh.

Aaron turned the doorknob—and it came off in his hand. "Hey!" he cried out in surprise.

The door creaked open. Aaron pushed it open all the way. We stared into the foggy gray light of the front hallway. A whiff of cold air washed over me. Cold, sour air.

I shuddered.

"Let's go in," Aaron whispered. He stepped inside and I followed him.

We took two or three steps into the dark hallway—and the front door slammed behind us.

5

I **JUMPED A MILE** into the air. "Hey—who *did* that?" I cried.

Aaron's eyes bulged behind his swim goggles. "M-maybe it was just the wind," he stammered.

I pulled a flashlight from my backpack and shone it around. We stepped into the living room. Our boots clanked noisily on the bare wooden floor. The furniture was all covered with yellowed bedsheets.

Aaron cupped his hands around his mouth. "Anyone home?" he shouted. His words echoed in the big empty room. "Hello? Any ghosts here?"

Silence.

"Duh. Good try," I said, rolling my eyes. "Ghosts always come out when you call them."

Aaron shrugged. "Whatever." He raised the camcorder and aimed it at himself. He pushed the Record button. "Saturday night. Twenty-one hundred hours. We have reached our destination and are ready to explore."

He pushed the button again. Then he turned to me. "Just setting the scene. You know."

I squinted at him. "It's nine o'clock. Why did you say twenty-one hundred hours?"

"I was trying to impress the ghosts," he replied.

I told you he's weird.

We started to explore the enormous living room. The sheets draped over the couches and chairs were thick with dust. I raised my light and saw a blanket of cobwebs hanging from the ceiling and clinging to one wall. Cobwebs covered the glass chandelier over the center of the room.

"No one has been in here for ages," I whispered.

A sound above our heads made us both gasp. Loud creaking.

"Hello? Is someone upstairs?" Aaron shouted. He raised his camcorder and aimed it toward the curving stairway at the back wall.

Silence now.

We moved into the next room, a dining room. A long table covered in a white tablecloth. At least, I *thought* it was a tablecloth—until I stepped closer. And saw that the table was actually covered with cobwebs.

"Hey!" I cried out as I stepped in something sticky.

"What's your problem? Did you find anything?" Aaron asked, hurrying over to me.

22

I lowered my flashlight to the floor—and saw that I had stepped into a sticky puddle of green goo.

"Ectoplasm!" Aaron declared. "Ghosts always leave ectoplasm behind."

"It's probably bubble gum," I said.

I mean, I had two real ghosts at home, and they didn't leave green goo behind everywhere they went.

Aaron bent down to study it. "Yes!" He pumped his fists in the air. "Definitely ectoplasm. This is proof. Quick, Max—put your boot back in the goo."

"Excuse me? You want me to—?"

"Hurry. I've got to get this on tape."

With a sigh, I stuck my boot back in the green goo. Aaron lowered the camcorder and taped a close-up. "First sighting," he said in a serious, deep voice. "First evidence that ghosts are here."

I unstuck myself and we moved to the next room—a large den with a broad stone fireplace against one wall. "We're getting close. I know it!" Aaron said.

"Aaron, don't get your hopes up," I said. I glanced at the cobwebs that covered the window like a shade. "It's just us and a million spiders."

But then we heard the creaking overhead again. The ceiling groaned. Wind made the window-panes rattle.

And from somewhere far away, I thought I heard laughter.

6

SOFT AT FIRST, THEN louder. Shrill laughter, like someone hitting the highest notes on a piano.

A chill ran down my back. I suddenly felt scared.

I turned to Aaron. "Did you hear that too?"

He stood frozen in front of the fireplace. "Where did it c-come from?" he stammered.

"I . . . don't know," I whispered.

We both stood perfectly still and listened. But the laughter had stopped.

Wind whistled through the windowpanes. Outside, a tree branch tapped hard against the window, as if trying to break in.

"Let's keep moving," Aaron said. He kept the camcorder raised as we walked quickly down a curving hall and into the next room.

The room seemed to stretch for miles. It was long and bare, except for a faded red carpet and a few scattered wooden chairs. I raised my light to the ceiling high above our heads. Six huge crystal chandeliers formed a line above our heads.

"Wow. This must have been a ballroom or something," I said. "You know. Like in a castle."

"Maybe the ghosts still come here and dance," Aaron said.

"Maybe," I said, shining my light around the floor.

I nearly dropped the flashlight when I heard the laughter again. Muffled this time, as if coming from behind a closet door.

Cold laughter. Shrill and sharp, like glass breaking.

Aaron and I spun around, expecting to see someone. No. No one.

"Who is it?" Aaron called out. "Who's there?"

Another burst of ugly laughter, farther away this time.

The laughter sent chill after chill down my back. If there were ghosts in this house, they definitely weren't friendly!

"It's coming from over there," Aaron said. He pointed to a doorway at the other end of the ballroom. "Let's go."

We made our way back into the long, curving hallway. Then we both stopped and looked around. "Which way did we come into the house?" I asked. "I'm all turned around."

"Me too," Aaron said. "This place is too big."

A blast of cold wind made me gasp. The air

felt wet and heavy on my cheeks. Where did it come from?

Another swirling gust made Aaron and me turn our backs to it. "Did someone leave a door open?" Aaron asked.

"It . . . isn't this windy outside," I said. "It's like a wind tunnel in here."

"The ghosts . . . ," Aaron said. "They don't want us to go that way. They're trying to keep us out."

The wind howled through the hallway, pushing us back. Aaron and I ducked into a small room. It was narrow and low-ceilinged, and it had no windows.

I shone my light around the room. My trembling hand made the light beam dance over the back wall.

The circle of light stopped on oozing green goo dripping down the wall. The floor beneath it was puddled with goo.

I swallowed, my mouth suddenly dry.

I didn't want to come here because I'd thought it was a waste of time. But now I wasn't so sure.

The high-pitched laughter . . . the creaking footsteps over our heads . . . the strange blasts of cold, wet wind . . . the green globs of sticky goo. Were there really ghosts here?

Aaron raised the camcorder and taped the oozing green stuff. "Ectoplasm caught on tape for the first time in recorded history," he said in a deep voice into the microphone. "Evidence that the ghosts we seek are close by. They may even be watching us now."

He turned the camcorder on me. "Max, are you scared?"

"Maybe a little," I said. "But I still don't think there are ghosts in this old house."

I didn't want to admit on the video how frightened I was.

I have real ghosts at home, I thought. But they're not scary.

I wanted to get out of there. Okay, I'm not the bravest person in the world. But I couldn't leave Aaron alone.

Teeth chattering, I took a deep breath and followed Aaron back into the hall. I tensed my body for the wind blasts. But the air was still now.

We turned and followed another hallway, which turned into another hallway and another.

"I'm kinda lost," Aaron said.

"Me too," I replied. "Maybe that's the kitchen." I pointed ahead.

We stepped into a square, low-ceilinged room. Gray light washed in from a dust-covered window. Big cartons were stacked along one wall.

"Just a big closet," Aaron murmured. He pulled up the lid of a carton and peered inside. "Yuck. Moldy old books. They're totally rotting."

27

I stepped up to a tall grandfather clock against one wall. As I raised the flashlight to its face, the slender black hands started to move. They both spun wildly, faster and faster.

"Oh!" I let out a startled cry and staggered back.

Aaron looked up from the carton of books. "What's wrong?"

"That clock—" I pointed. "Uh . . ." Now the hands were perfectly still. "Nothing," I muttered. "Forget it. Guess I'm just a little creeped out."

I turned away from the clock. My flashlight stopped on a long box near the window. Whoa. Wait. Not a box.

"Aaron—" I whispered. "Look. Is that a coffin?"

He spun around, eyes wide.

Yes. A long, black coffin, polished and shiny. We stepped over to it.

"Do you think there's someone in it?" Aaron asked. "Who would keep a coffin in a storage closet?"

"A vampire," I said.

"We don't want a vampire," Aaron said. "We're doing ghosts."

I stared at the lid. The wood was smooth and shiny, reflecting the gray light from the window.

"Open it," Aaron said. "Go ahead."

"Whoa. No way," I told him. "*You* open it."

"I'm holding the camcorder," he replied. "I

have to tape what happens. Go ahead. Open the lid."

I jammed my hands into my parka pockets. "I don't think so."

Aaron sighed. "Come on, Max. You don't want to do the history of Paraguay, do you? Open the lid. We're going to get an A here. I just know it."

I stared at the brass handles on the lid. My legs were trembling. My heart pounded in my chest. Paraguay was starting to sound pretty good.

"Go ahead. I'm taping," Aaron said.

I pulled my hands from the parka. I moved closer to the coffin. I reached for the handles.

Slowly, slowly, I began to pull up the coffin lid. I lifted it an inch . . . two inches . . .

And the lid shot open!

Without warning, a grinning skeleton leaped up, bones clattering. Before I could move, it stretched out its arms—and made a grab for me.

I heard Aaron's scream of horror behind me.

And then my scream rose over his. My trembling legs collapsed.

And I fell facedown into the coffin!

7

I LET OUT ANOTHER horrified cry. Somehow I pushed myself up to my knees. Then I scrambled out of the coffin. My heart pounded so hard, my chest hurt. I staggered back, gasping for breath.

Grinning at me, the skeleton rattled and shook. I saw the deep empty sockets where its eyes had been.

And then I saw the metal rod holding the skeleton up. And the coiled springs that had made it stand.

"It . . . it's a total fake," I said.

The skeleton stood still now, arms at its sides, head slumped at an angle.

"Yeah. It's a jack-in-the-box thing," Aaron said. "Like in a carnival fun house. I knew it."

I spun around. "Oh, right. You knew it? If you knew it, why did you scream?"

He patted his camcorder. "For the tape. You know. To make it more dramatic. I only screamed for the tape."

I still hadn't caught my breath. "You got it all

on tape? Me screaming and falling into the coffin and everything?"

He laughed. "Yeah. I got it."

"Maybe we'll have to edit that part out," I said.

"Yeah, maybe," Aaron said. "I mean, you're the class brain, right? Everyone calls you Brainimon because you're so smart. No one wants to see the smartest kid in the class shaking like a leaf and falling face-first into a coffin—do they?"

He laughed again. He was enjoying this too much!

I was thinking hard. If the skeleton was fake, the rest of the eerie sounds must be fake too.

"I'm outta here," I said. "This is a big waste of time."

I started toward the door. Aaron chased me and grabbed me by the shoulder. "What's the chief export of Paraguay?" he asked. "What's the national flower? How do their elections work?"

"Okay, okay. I'm staying," I said.

We stepped into the hall and found ourselves at a steep stairway that led upstairs. "I know there are ghosts in this house," Aaron said. "They're probably hiding in the bedrooms up here."

The stairs creaked and groaned under our boots. Part of the railing had broken away. At the top, we faced a long, narrow hall with closed doors on both sides.

The glass had broken away in the window at

the end of the hall. Flimsy white curtains blew in the breeze, waving to us like ghostly figures.

I felt a chill. I had a heavy feeling in the pit of my stomach. Something was warning me that there was *real* danger nearby.

Aaron and I stepped into the first bedroom. The room was big and cluttered with furniture—a canopy bed, a long dresser, armchairs, and a couch. Everything was covered with dust. The room smelled like stale cigarette smoke.

Heavy drapes covered the windows. I moved my light along the wall—and stopped at a narrow door. I pulled open the door and peered into another hall. A secret hallway!

"Hey, Aaron, check this out." I kept the light down on the floor ahead of us as we crept into this new hallway. There were no lights or windows. It was like a low, narrow tunnel.

I held back. It reminded me of the creepy tunnel I'd found behind my bedroom wall. The tunnel that led from the living . . . to the world of ghosts.

I'd gone into that terrifying tunnel once. I never wanted to go in there again.

I shivered. This is a different tunnel, I told myself. It's not even a tunnel. It's just a hallway in an empty old house.

"Let's go," I said.

Our footsteps echoed loudly as we hurried

through it, keeping close together. The hall ended at a small alcove with three doors side by side.

"This is excellent!" Aaron said. He was video-ing the whole thing. "Hidden rooms at the end of a hidden hallway. Awesome."

The first door seemed to be locked from the inside. Aaron couldn't get the door to budge, so he tried the middle door, and it opened easily.

We stepped into a huge room cluttered with cartons, stacks of old children's books, a beat-up wooden baby crib, an old-fashioned bike, and piles of old clothes. "Check it out!" Aaron exclaimed. He bent to search through a stack of old comic books.

A long time ago, this must have been a children's room. I saw a pile of board games against the wall. The boxes were faded and torn. I started to pick up the game on top—Parcheesi.

But a sound behind me made me drop it and spin around. "Aaron, did you hear that? Like a howling sound?"

I listened hard and heard it again. A long, low howl, like a dog in pain. And then I heard a sharp tapping on the door.

Had we closed the door? I thought we'd left it open.

Another tap on the door. And then knocking sounds *coming from the wall*!

My fear tightened every muscle in my body. I

forced myself to breathe. "Aaron—what's up with that?" I turned back to him. "Hey—Aaron? Do you hear it?"

I didn't see him.

The howl rose, louder now, as if it was right behind me in the room. And now the tapping came from all four walls. *Taptap taptaptap*—surrounding me!

"Hey, I don't like this," I said. I ran over to the stack of old comics. "Aaron? Where are you?"

I swept my light around the cartons and piles of old clothes. "Aaron? Come on—answer me! Is this a joke or something? It isn't funny."

I couldn't find him. Why didn't he answer?

"Hey, Aaron? Aaron?"

8

PANIC WASHED OVER ME. I swept the light rapidly around the room. "Aaron! Aaron!" No answer. No sign of him.

Howl after howl rang in my ears. The pounding on the walls grew louder and louder, as if a hundred people were banging on the other side, banging to be let in.

I turned to run—and stumbled over a wooden dollhouse. I tumbled to my knees. Trembling, I started to stand up. "Ohh." I let out a cry as I felt something brush my cheek. Something cold and soft.

"No, please—" Something cold touched the back of my neck. Icy fingers. Invisible. "Please—"

The room grew colder. The howls rose and fell. I felt something warm plop onto my shoulder.

"Ohh." I glanced down. It was a glob of green goo.

I raised my eyes. Thick green goo dripped from the ceiling and slid down the walls. As it dripped, it hissed with steam, hot against the cold air.

35

"Aaron—where are you?" I screamed over the steady drumming on the walls.

And then floating above me, I saw a face. A woman's face, long white hair trailing from her head. Her eyes shut tight. The face flickered above me. Whoa. Wait. Her eyes weren't shut. They were missing! I gasped in horror—and she faded away.

I spun to the door. I knew I had to get out of there.

I tried to run. But icy hands tightened around my shoulders and held me in place.

The hissing green goo pooled around me on the floor. And an arm floated just over my head. A pale skinny arm without a body.

It vanished and was replaced by two bare legs and a foot. Floating . . . floating in the cold air. The foot had no toes! The toes had been sliced off. I could see the dark scabs at the end of it.

The foot vanished and a man appeared, sad-looking, staring down at me with pleading eyes. Hands reached for me. I saw several people floating under the dripping ceiling, all sad, all pale, their mouths moving as if they were trying to talk to me.

A hand shot out and grabbed for the silver pendant around my neck. The pendant is shaped like a bullet. My mother found it when we moved into our house, and she gave it to me for good luck.

With a cry, I jerked back. The hand wrapped tightly around my pendant and started to pull.

"No!" I slapped it away.

I spun around, holding the pendant with both hands.

"Aaron—where are you?"

The howls turned to moans. The drumming on the walls became deafening. My boots stuck in the thick hot goo. I gazed up at the sad, damaged faces and bodies moving so slowly, as if in a nightmare.

But this is real, I thought. Horribly real.

I was shivering from the cold. My teeth were chattering. Icy fingers brushed my cheeks.

I lurched away from them. Tugged and tugged—and finally unstuck my boots from the thick green ooze—and staggered to the door. I grabbed the knob and pulled it hard. To my surprise, the door opened easily. Back in the hidden hallway I ran, leaving the howls and drumming behind.

I turned a corner, breathing hard. Someone stood hunched in a doorway. A dark figure.

I stopped. And raised my light.

Aaron?

"Aaron, where did you go?"

"Nowhere. I was in that kids' room. With you."

"No, you weren't. I looked for you," I said. "How did you get out here?"

He shook his head groggily. "I . . . don't really

remember. I was looking for you, Max. I couldn't seem to find you anywhere."

I pointed toward the room. "Real g-ghosts," I stammered. "You missed them. Real ones."

"No way," Aaron said. "This whole place is a fake. You were right, Max."

I didn't want to argue. I just wanted to get *out*.

We ran to the end of the hidden hallway, out the narrow door, down another long, dimly lit hall. We found the stairway and took the steps down two at a time.

I didn't look back. I didn't want to see anything following me.

Curtains fluttered in a strong breeze over a broken window. The floor creaked beneath us as we ran.

The front door!

I reached it first, gasping for breath, my side aching. I grabbed the knob and yanked the door open.

"No!" I let out a cry of disappointment. Not the front door. A closet.

I turned away and started to run again—but something caught my eye. Something shiny on the closet floor.

I bent down to investigate. And saw a pile of silver objects. Bullet-shaped objects. Just like the one I wore around my neck.

What were they doing in this closet?

I grabbed a bunch and shoved them into my parka pocket. Then I started to run again.

"Hey, Max—slow down," Aaron called. "What's your hurry?"

"I want to get *out* of here!" I shouted.

The halls twisted and curved. We ran past the dining room, a den we hadn't seen, the huge ballroom—and found ourselves back at the dining room.

Or was it a *different* dining room?

"Are . . . are we going around in circles?" Aaron asked, gasping for breath.

"I think . . . that way," I said, pointing.

We trotted down another hall with rooms on both sides. A dark wooden door came into view at the end. Yes! This had to be the front door.

I recognized the entryway. "This is where we came in," I said. "And this is where we go out!"

I grabbed the knob, turned it, and pulled.

The door didn't budge. I tried again.

Then I tried pushing.

No way.

And then I heard the eerie, terrifying howls in the hall behind us. Growing louder. Coming closer.

Frantically, I turned the knob and struggled with the door. And then with a hoarse sigh, I turned to Aaron. "We're locked in," I said. "We're trapped in here."

9

AARON HAD BEEN PLAYING it cool, saying everything in the house was a fake. But I saw his expression change, and I heard his rapid breathing. He was afraid too. He grabbed the doorknob and yanked with all his strength.

We both gasped when the door flew open.

Aaron burst out into the snow, and I followed close behind. Back in the house, I could hear the eerie howls that had chased us through the halls.

"Yes! We're out! We're out!" I cried happily. My heart was racing. I dropped to my knees in the snow, took a deep breath, and held it, trying to calm down.

Aaron packed a big snowball between his hands and heaved it at the house. It splattered against the shingles over the front stoop.

"Did you enjoy my haunted house?"

Startled by the voice, I turned and saw a young man smiling down at me. His hands were jammed into the pockets of a long gray overcoat, and he had a black fur hat perched over long blond hair.

"Uh . . . hi," I said, scrambling to my feet. Aaron had another snowball in his hands. But he let it drop to the ground.

"Kinda late for you boys, isn't it?" the man said. "I didn't see you go in." His bright blue eyes studied us. "It's not really open yet."

"Open?" I said. What was he talking about?

He nodded. "The haunted house. I'm not going to open for another week or two."

Aaron and I both stared at him. "You mean—?"

"I bought the Grover Mansion last fall," he said. "My name is Martin Morgo. When I moved to town, a lot of people told me stories about the house being haunted, and I thought it would be a good tourist attraction. So I bought it and—"

"But—but—" I sputtered. "There are *real* ghosts in there! I saw them. I felt them. It's not just ghost stories. They're *real*!"

Mr. Morgo laughed. "Fantastic special effects, huh? I had some Hollywood guys come out and work on it. They were expensive, but they did a great job."

I opened my mouth but no sound came out. Was he kidding me? Did I let myself get terrified by a bunch of movie special effects?

Mr. Morgo stared at me. "You didn't think it was *too* scary, did you?"

"Oh no. No way," I lied. "It was . . . way cool."

He smiled. "That's good. Because I want little kids to be able to enjoy it too."

"Well . . . the goo dripping down the walls and the ceiling—that was pretty scary," I said.

He nodded. "Yeah. You're right. Do you know we had to install a really powerful spraying system to clean the room each time we do that effect?"

"Awesome," I said. I glanced at Aaron. I think we were both starting to feel pretty stupid for getting scared at a fake haunted house.

Morgo shivered and turned to Aaron. "How come you're wearing shorts in this freezing cold weather?"

Aaron shrugged. "Beats me. I just like shorts."

Morgo blinked. "Well, come again, guys. Okay? Thanks for testing it out." He shook hands with us. His hand was surprisingly hot. "You boys should get home. It's nearly eleven o'clock."

Aaron and I started clomping through the snow toward the sidewalk.

"Tell your friends about it, guys!" Morgo shouted after us. "Tell 'em how terrifying it is—okay?"

The snow had stopped coming down, but the wind blew the icy flakes into our faces. Clouds covered the moon. I pulled up my parka hood and leaned into the wind as we walked to the bus stop.

Aaron jogged to keep up with me. He laughed.

"Max, you're the one who's totally into ghosts and haunted houses. How could you believe that stuff was real? The whole place was totally fake."

I heard Aaron's question, but I didn't answer. I was staring behind us, staring at the snow in front of the Grover mansion.

The snow had totally *melted* where Morgo had stood!

10

MONDAY AFTERNOON, AARON AND I still had the Grover Mansion on our minds.

"Look, Max—another ghost!" Aaron pointed to a big snowdrift and laughed. "Ghosts! Everywhere you look!"

I didn't like Aaron making fun of me about ghosts. I mean, I knew the truth about ghosts, and he didn't.

As we walked home from school, he kept talking about what a sucker I was for believing the special effects in the haunted house. Finally, I couldn't take it anymore. I decided to tell Aaron the whole story of how I really was haunted. And this time I wouldn't leave anything out. This time I'd make him believe me.

I told him about Nicky and Tara. How they showed up because they used to live in my house. How they're dead, they're ghosts and they don't know why, and they don't know where their parents are. And how I'm the only one who can see them. And how they want me to help them find their parents.

I told Aaron the whole story. It just spilled out of me. I don't think I took a breath. And then I stopped walking and turned to him. And I said, "Well? Do you believe me?"

I waited . . . waited for his answer.

He stared at me through his swim goggles. And finally, he said, "Yes. I believe you, Max."

I was so happy—for about three seconds.

Because then Aaron added, "And guess what? Godzilla lives in my basement. I sneak food down to him all the time."

He laughed so hard, he fell backward into the snow. Howling at the top of his lungs, he rolled around and around in the snow, very pleased with his dumb joke.

Oh, well.

Aaron is my best friend. But I guess you can't expect best friends to believe everything you say.

Heavy clouds lowered in the afternoon sky. It was dark as night. The streetlights had come on early. They made the snow sparkle.

We reached Aaron's block. "When are you going to return the camcorder?" he asked. I had borrowed it after the haunted house disaster.

"You can have it back tomorrow," I said. "I just want to check out what's on it. You know, you left it on. You were so scared, you forgot to stop recording."

"I wasn't scared," Aaron said. "I wanted to capture every moment on video."

Yeah, sure.

I waved good-bye to Aaron, turned onto my street, and started to jog. I was cold from head to foot. I rubbed my nose to try to get some feeling into it.

I checked my watch. I couldn't wait until five o'clock. I had a study date with Traci Wayne. An actual study date with the most beautiful, most popular, most *awesome* girl in school—maybe in the universe!

That morning, Traci had stopped me in the hall at school and asked if she could come over. I was so excited, I couldn't speak. I had to write my answer on the wall.

Traci Wayne in my house? Did that mean she *liked* me?

My house came into view across the street. I started to cross over—then a sharp blast of pain shot through my body.

Something smashed hard into the back of my head.

I staggered forward for a step or two. Then my legs gave way, and I fell facedown into the deep snow.

11

THE PAIN SLOWLY FADED. I heard laughter behind me.

I raised my head from the snow, slowly turned—and saw the two worst kids at Jefferson Elementary. Willy and Billy, the Wilbur brothers.

These two brothers are big, freckle-faced, redheaded, blubber-bellied, fat-fisted, boneheaded tough guys. Everyone hates them. Even their parents can't stand them. They make Billy and Willy sleep in the garage.

For some reason, the Wilbur brothers are always in my face.

At school, they like to run up behind me in the hall and jerk my shirt up out of my pants. They give me really painful wedgies in the locker room before every gym class. They trip me on the stairs and when I'm carrying a tray in the lunchroom.

I know they're the ones who filled my locker up to the top with boiling-hot water. I can't prove it, but I know it was the Wilburs.

And now here they were, giggling and hee-hawing at the top of their lungs and heaving ice balls at me right outside my house.

I struggled to my knees. "Hey, guys. How's it going?" I always try to treat them as human, even though they're from a lower species.

Billy ran up and smashed a snowball into my face, grinding it to powder.

They high-fived each other. "You like snow, right, Max?" Willy asked, grinning at me, his piggy black eyes glowing. He and his brother took me by the shoulders and dragged me over to a low hedge by the curb.

"Here." Billy scooped some snow into his gloves. "Eat some of this. It's real tasty."

I tried to pull back, but they held my head. "What is it?" I croaked.

"Yellow snow," Billy said. "Your favorite."

"Hey—no way!" I cried. I stared at the heap of snow in his hands. It was totally drenched with yellow.

"Eat it," Billy Wilbur said. "It's good. Yellow snow is the best!"

I turned my face away. I tried to squirm free. And out of the corner of my eye, I saw Nicky and Tara. They stood in my neighbors' yard, leaning on two big snowmen, watching me struggle.

"Help me!" I called.

The Wilbur brothers laughed. "No one here to

help you, Brainimon. Come on, eat. It's got vitamins and minerals."

"Couldn't we maybe talk about this?" I said, watching Nicky and Tara. "My doctor says yellow snow might be fattening."

"Funny," Billy said, pushing the disgusting stuff toward my face. "But you know what's funnier? You eating yellow snow."

I watched Nicky and Tara bend down and start to make snowballs.

"Hey, guys—check it out," I said to the Wilburs. I pointed to the snowmen.

The Wilbur brothers raised their eyes—and saw snowballs come flying at them.

"Whoa!"

"No way!"

Billy dropped the disgusting yellow snow. Willy let go of me and took a step back. The two snowmen grinned at us as snowballs flew one after the other.

"What's up with *that*?" Billy cried.

A snowball thudded to the ground at Willy's feet.

Billy's mouth dropped open. "Who's throwing those snowballs? It c-can't be the snowmen!"

They forgot about me and took off running. Kicking up snow, bumping into each other, they bleated like two stampeding water buffaloes.

Nicky and Tara floated over to me, and we watched the Wilburs run. "Nice work," I said.

But Billy Wilbur turned at the corner. He scooped up snow—and heaved a fat snowball at me.

"Hey—"

Smack. The snowball hit Tara in the face.

She staggered back a few steps, then raised her hands to her cheeks and started to scream. "Ow! It burns! It's burning hot! Help me! My face—it *burns!*"

I grabbed Tara, spun her around, and gasped. Her face was red as fire!

12

I RUBBED MOST OF the snow off Tara's face with my glove. Then Nicky and I helped her into the house.

It was nearly five o'clock. Everyone was home.

Mom was in the kitchen. I could smell something good baking. The basement door stood open, and I could hear Dad and my older brother, Colin, having one of their Ping-Pong wars.

Ping-Pong isn't a game with them—it's a contact sport. They smash the ball at each other and try to knock each other over. They crush about a dozen balls a game and usually knock out a few teeth, and think it's great fun.

My dad is a big loud red-faced Mack truck of a guy with a tattoo of a fire-eating dragon on one arm. It's perfect—because Dad *acts* like a fire-breathing dragon too.

He and Colin get along great because Colin is tall and good-looking, and popular, and a big sports star—in other words, perfect in every way.

I'm perfect in *other* ways. But only Mom seems to notice.

Anyway, Nicky and I led Tara up to my room. I got a towel and gently wiped the rest of the snow off her face. Her cheeks were still bright red, but her skin didn't burn as much.

"I don't get it," she said, shaking her head. "Suddenly I'm allergic to *snow*?"

I tossed the towel into the corner and dropped onto the edge of my bed. "Well, I'm allergic to *yellow* snow," I said. "Thanks for rescuing me, guys."

Nicky sat down beside me. He slapped my back. "Now we need you to rescue *us*, old buddy."

"We're desperate," Tara said. "We've got to find our parents. Nicky and I have tried everything."

"We're feeling weak," Nicky said. "We keep appearing and disappearing. We can't control it."

"And we really miss them," Tara said, her voice breaking. She tugged at one of the dangling red earrings she always wore. She always did that when she was really upset. "I'm so worried about them, Max. Where could they be?"

I gazed back at her. I didn't know what to say. I felt so bad for them.

"We have a new clue," Tara said. "Lulu said something, but we don't understand what it means. She said, 'Colder than the grave.' That's all. 'Colder than the grave.'"

I shook my head. What could that mean?

"We need a plan," Nicky said. "You've got to help us—"

"Whoa." I jumped up when I glimpsed the clock. "I can't help you right now, guys," I said. "Can we talk about it later?"

Tara narrowed her eyes at me. "Later?"

"I have to get ready. I have a five o'clock study date with Traci Wayne. She'll be here any second," I said, feeling my heart start to pound.

I don't know if I'm in love with Traci or just have a major crush or what. But every time I see her, my heart starts to beat a hip-hop rhythm, my skin starts to tingle and break out in a rash, and my tongue ties itself into knots and hangs down to my chin.

Is that true love, do you think?

Traci is blond and pretty, not in a stuck-up way. She is in the totally cool group at school. And I am in the fungus life group.

So when she came up to me in school and asked to come over, you can imagine my shock. But I played it cool. I only did *two* backward cartwheels.

I hurried to my mirror. I tried to brush down my hair. But it's thick and curly, and it always pops right back up. Colin says it looks like I'm wearing a small brown poodle on my head.

Nice guy.

"Don't be nervous, Max," Tara said. She stood behind me, but she had no reflection in the mirror.

"Don't be nervous?" I cried. "This is Traci Wayne!"

"But we'll be right there to help you," Nicky said.

"No way!" I cried. "I don't want your help. We'll talk later. Okay?"

I changed into my coolest T-shirt—dark gray, with the words WHUSSUP, DAWG? in red. Then I hurried downstairs. "Hey, Mom," I said to her in the kitchen.

She was sliding a tray of cookies from the oven. I took a long, deep breath. Wow.

"Toll House. Your favorite," she said, setting the tray on the counter. "I thought you might need milk and cookies for your study date."

"You're the best, Mom," I said. It always makes her smile when I say something like that. Mom usually looks kinda sad and tense. Maybe it's because she's a tiny quiet person and she's married to a big loud elephant.

That could make you kinda tense, don't you think?

Dad and Colin came up from the basement, sweaty and red-faced. Dad said he was going out to shovel the driveway.

Colin stepped up to me with a big grin on his

face. He opened his mouth and spit a Ping-Pong ball at me.

"Hey!" It bounced off my forehead.

"One to nothing, my favor," Colin said.

"Leave Maxie alone," Mom told him. "He has a study date. And I don't want you playing your usual tricks and trying to embarrass Max when his friend is here."

"No problem," Colin said. But I didn't believe him. He's always de-pantsing me or something when my friends come over.

"Yo! Cookies!" he cried.

"Those are for Max and Traci," Mom said.

"Yeah, sure," Colin said. He grabbed two steaming cookies off the tray and stuffed them into his mouth.

Colin chewed for a few seconds—and then his eyes bulged. "Hot!" he gasped. "H-hot!" He opened his mouth and the cookies came spewing out—all down the front of my new T-shirt.

"Stop picking on Maxie," Mom said.

The doorbell rang.

Traci!

The coolest girl in school in *my* house!

My heart did a flip-flop. I felt sweat pop out all over my forehead. I hurried to the front door and pulled it open.

Please, please—let this study date go well!

13

TRACI STOOD ON THE front stoop in a red down jacket and brown suede Ugg boots. She had a smile on her face as I opened the door. But her smile faded quickly.

"Ooh, gross," she said. "What's that brown gook on your shirt? Did you barf or something?"

"Heeh heeh," I said. My tongue was suddenly as big as a salami.

Not a good start.

I brushed most of the cookie barf off and stepped back so Traci could come in.

Mom said hi and hung Traci's jacket in the front closet. Then Traci carried her backpack into the kitchen, and we sat down at the table.

Mom served the cookies and milk.

Traci pulled books and a notebook from her bag. "Have you started your social studies project?" she asked.

"Heeh heeh," I replied.

She stared at me, waiting for a better answer.

I took a deep breath. I knew I could untangle my tongue if I really tried.

"Well, Aaron and I are supposed to do the history of Paraguay," I said, finally getting my mouth to work. "But we went to the Grover Mansion Saturday night. And maybe we're going to do something about ghosts instead."

Traci laughed. "A haunted house? How come you're so into ghosts, Max?"

I couldn't tell her the real reason.

I couldn't tell her that I had two ghosts waiting for me in my bedroom right now.

I shrugged. "I'm just into it."

Traci tossed back her straight blond hair. "Do you really believe in ghosts?"

"Kinda," I said. "The Grover Mansion—I guess it was pretty fake. But it had great special effects. I mean, the ghosts seemed real."

"Ms. McDonald won't let you do a project on ghosts," Traci said. "Ghosts aren't social studies." She took a bite of a cookie and got a smear of chocolate on her perfect chin. I didn't know if I should tell her about it or not.

"I brought my math problems," she said, opening her notebook. She flashed me a smile. "Think you could do them for me, Brain-imon?"

Oh, wow.

So *that's* why she wanted to come over. It wasn't a study date. She just wanted me to do her math problems for her.

I sighed.

"Max, what's that pendant?"

The silver pendant I wear around my neck had swung loose. Traci grabbed it to study it. "That's awesome."

"My mom found it and gave it to me," I said. "You really like it?"

She nodded.

"Hey, wait," I said. "I'll show you something." I hurried to the front closet, pulled the six silver-bullet-shaped objects from my parka pocket, and trotted back to the kitchen table.

"Check these out." I spread them on the table. "I found these in the haunted house. Look. They match mine. Isn't that weird?"

Traci studied the six silver objects. She picked two of them up and rolled them around in her hand. "Know what, Max? These are just what I need for the necklace I'm making."

"Really?" Wow. I suddenly had an easy way to impress Traci Wayne. How many days and nights had I daydreamed about this moment?

"Take them," I said. I rolled all six of them over to her. "Take them. They're all yours."

"Hey—thank you, Max!"

I had a big smile on my face as I watched Traci tuck the six objects into her bag.

Of course, I had no way of knowing that I had just put us both in deadly danger.

14

"**NOW LET'S TAKE A** look at the math problems," I said.

Traci slid the book and her notebook over to me. "You're so good at long equations," she said. "I always lose my place halfway through."

I studied the page of problems. I'd already done this page and handed it in. "Would you like me to explain them to you?" I asked. "Or just do them?"

"Just do them," Traci answered.

I picked up a pencil and started to work on the first problem. But I didn't get very far because Colin came dancing into the room.

And what was he holding up in front of him? A pair of white underpants.

Colin had a fat, disgusting grin on his face. "Are these yours, Max?" he asked, holding the underpants up by the elastic. "How did they get in my dresser drawer?"

He waved them in front of Traci.

She put a hand over her mouth and giggled.

I could feel my face turning red-hot and knew I

was blushing. Colin was just trying to embarrass me—and it was working!

Colin raised the underpants to his face and sniffed them. A long, loud sniff. "Yep. They're yours!" he said. He laughed and tossed the underpants from hand to hand.

With her hand covering her mouth, Traci giggled some more.

I wanted to sink under the table and never come up. Why was Colin doing this to me?

Because he's Colin, that's why.

Colin started to dance around the room, waving the underpants above his head like a flag.

"Colin—please!" I shouted. I blinked as Nicky and Tara appeared in the doorway.

They stopped Colin and spun him around. His eyes bulged. He didn't know *what* was going on.

Tara grabbed the underpants from Colin's hand—and jammed them down over his head.

Traci let out a cry. She couldn't see Nicky and Tara. All she could see was the underpants leaping out of Colin's hands and flying down over his face.

Then Nicky grabbed the elastic of Colin's underpants and gave him a screaming wedgie.

Both ghosts shoved Colin hard. He stumbled from the kitchen with the underpants over his head.

Traci squinted at me across the table. "Max, I'm confused. Why did your brother *do* that?"

"He's very immature," I said.

We turned back to the math problems. I hoped that was the last of Colin. "When we finish, maybe I can show you some of my new magic tricks," I said. "Mom bought me a live rabbit, and I've been practicing making it appear and disappear."

Traci glanced at her watch. "No. I don't think so. I have to get to Patti Berger's party. Are you going?"

I kept my eyes on the math problems. "I wasn't invited," I said. "Patti doesn't know I'm alive."

"Yes, she does," Traci replied. "She just doesn't like you."

I glanced over Traci's shoulder and saw Nicky and Tara at the kitchen counter. They were helping themselves to cookies and milk.

Please don't turn around, Traci, I thought.

Too late. Traci turned to see what I was staring at.

"Oh, wow!" She leaped to her feet. "Those cookies!" she screamed. "They're flying back and forth. And the milk is spilling in midair! Max, what's going on?"

"No problem," I said. "It's just a snack attack."

Traci grabbed all her stuff, jammed it into her

backpack, and took off, heading for the front door. "You're too weird!" she shouted. "Your brother is weird! Your house is weird! You're *all* weird!"

The front door slammed behind her. She was gone.

I sat staring at the bare table. "This didn't happen," I murmured.

Mom poked her head in. "Maxie? How did your study date go?"

I searched for Nicky and Tara, but they had disappeared again. I spotted the camcorder on my bed. I rewound the tape, fell back on my bed, and started to watch it in the viewfinder.

I watched Aaron and me walking up to the Grover Mansion. And there we were inside the house. The picture was pretty good, even though it was so dark there.

I watched us exploring the living room, then moving to other rooms. Aaron was a good photographer. He kept the camcorder very still.

The tape wasn't very interesting. Until I got to a certain part. And then I jumped to my feet and nearly dropped the camcorder.

My hands were shaking. I watched the tape in the little viewfinder with my mouth hanging open in shock.

Just as the tape ended, Nicky and Tara

appeared in front of me. "Max, we've got to talk," Tara said. "You have to help us. We have to find our parents, and we're all out of ideas."

I lowered the camcorder and stared at the two ghosts. "You're not going to believe this," I said. "But I think I just found a big clue."

15

I REWOUND THE TAPE and started it again.

"Aaron and I went to this haunted house on the other side of town Saturday night," I explained. "We saw a lot of weird ghosts, and some strange things happened. Like eerie howls following us around and warm goo dripping down the walls. That kind of thing. But it was all a big fake."

Tara stared at the viewfinder. "You mean it was like a carnival fun house?"

"Yeah," I said. "Just special effects. That's what the owner told us."

"You met the owner?" Nicky asked.

"He was outside when we came running out of the house," I said. "He said his name is Morgo. He explained that he spent a lot of money on special effects. And he's going to open the haunted house soon. You know. And charge admission."

Tara narrowed her eyes at me. "So what's the big clue you found?"

"Keep watching the tape," I said.

"But I don't see anything," Tara said, frowning at the tiny screen. "It's just a dark empty room with nothing going on."

"That's right," I said. "Nothing going on. Now watch this part."

I fast-forwarded the tape to when Aaron and I came running out of the house and met Mr. Morgo. Aaron forgot to stop the camcorder, so it kept recording.

"What do you see?" I asked the two ghosts.

They both squinted into the viewfinder.

"I don't see anything but snow," Nicky said. "It's all just white."

"And there *you* are, Max," Tara said. "It looks like you're talking to someone—but no one's there."

"You've got *that* right!" I said. I tossed the camcorder down. "Aaron and I were talking to Mr. Morgo. But he doesn't show up on the tape. You can't see him and you can't hear him."

Nicky's eyes went wide. "You mean—?"

"You can't see any of the ghosts, either," I continued. "We saw ghosts all over the house. And Aaron had his camcorder recording the whole time. If they were just special-effects ghosts, they'd show up on the video, right?"

"So they were *real* ghosts!" Tara exclaimed.

"You got it," I said. "I think real ghosts live there. And Mr. Morgo was trying to hide that by telling us it was all special effects."

Nicky began pacing back and forth. Tara stared at the camcorder.

I could see they were both thinking hard.

"Your parents were scientists, right?" I said. "And they found a way to capture evil ghosts. They put them in some kind of prison."

"That's right," Nicky said. "But what does that have to do with these ghosts?"

"Try to follow me, here," I continued. "One of the evil ghosts found a way to escape. His name was Phears, and he was the most evil ghost. He let out all the other ghosts. But we don't know what happened to them. And we don't know what happened to your mom and dad."

Tara nodded, concentrating on what I was saying.

"Well, what if the Grover Mansion is where Phears' ghosts are hiding?" I said. "A haunted house is the perfect hiding place for a ghost, right?"

Tara's eyes flashed. I could see she was excited. "Those ghosts could help us," she said. "They can probably tell us how to find our parents."

Nicky grabbed his sister and spun her around. "But they're evil, Tara. Remember? These are totally evil, frightening ghosts. They won't help us. They'll probably try to hurt us. They'll—"

"Nicky, we have no choice," Tara said softly. "We have to go there."

16

TUESDAY AFTER SCHOOL, I ran home. I wanted to practice my magic act.

It had been snowing all day, and now it started to come down hard. I gazed out my bedroom window at the swirling flakes. Near the curb, I saw the two snowmen that Nicky and Tara had hidden behind when they bombed the Wilbur brothers with snowballs.

I snickered, thinking about how the Wilburs ran away screaming. Maybe they'll leave me alone now, I thought.

Oh, yeah. For sure.

I hadn't seen Nicky and Tara all day. Did they hurry over to the haunted house this morning? Would they go there without me?

No, they wouldn't, I decided. They'll come and get me when they're ready to go.

I set up my stand with the top hat and my other stuff. Then I gently grabbed Benny's ears and lifted him from his cage.

I know, I know. Benny is a lame name for a

bunny. Benny the Bunny. Puke, right? But that's only a *temporary* name until I can think of a good one.

I slipped Benny inside the top hat and petted his head. I loved his soft fur. "Relax, Benny," I whispered. "You've got the easy job."

Colin burst into the room. He had his parka on with the hood pulled over his head. He carried a big blue plastic disk under his arm.

"Going sledding?" I asked.

"No. Sunbathing," he said. He tromped over to me in his heavy snow boots and peered down at Benny inside the top hat. "Hey, the inside of my hood is made of rabbit fur."

"Shut up," I said. "Don't upset Benny." I pushed Colin back an inch. "Who are you sledding with?"

"Friends," Colin said. "You probably don't know that word, do you, Fat Face?"

"Don't call me Fat Face."

"Where *is* your one and only friend today?" Colin asked.

"Aaron? He's grounded."

"Oh, yeah? What did he do? Spit up his strained peas?"

"He gave his sister's favorite Barbie doll a tan."

"A suntan?"

"Yeah. In the microwave," I said. "It was a science experiment."

Colin snickered. He poked Benny with his gloved finger. "*Aaron* is a science experiment," he said. "A science experiment that went wrong."

"Don't poke Benny," I said.

"Okay." Colin swung his hand and poked me hard in the stomach. I doubled over, gasping.

He started for the door. "Fat Face, did you eat that chocolate chip muffin for breakfast?" he asked.

"Yeah," I said, rubbing my stomach.

"Well, bad news. Those weren't chocolate chips. They were rabbit pellets. I switched them before you woke up."

I gagged twice. "Thanks for telling me," I said.

But he was already out the door.

I turned back to Benny, who was crouched at the bottom of the top hat, his pink nose twitching like crazy. "Just chill," I told him. "I do all the hard work. You just sit there." The rabbit stared up at me as if he was trying to understand what I was telling him.

"First I show the audience that the hat is empty," I said. "Benny, you hide under the false bottom. Then I put the hat back on the table and I pull you out like this."

Gently, I grabbed Benny by the ears and lifted him from the hat. I held him high so that my imaginary audience could see him. I pictured my audience going wild, clapping, maybe giving me a standing ovation. I took a deep bow.

Then I started to lower Benny back into the hat.

Only he wouldn't go.

His ears—they were sticky. They stuck to the palm of my hand.

"Hey—what's up, Benny?" I grabbed the rabbit's middle and gave it a tug. The ears felt soft and hot, like melted candle wax. They stuck to my hand.

I tugged again. Benny's head stretched. I saw his white fur droop and melt.

"Oh no!" I let out a cry as the rabbit's head came off in my hand. Melting like hot wax, the white fur dripped as the body sank to the table in a steaming puddle.

"No—oh, please!" I cried, staring in horror at the melting rabbit head stuck to my hand. "What is *happening*?"

17

I FELT SICK. MY stomach lurched. I struggled to keep my breakfast down.

I tugged at the waxy rabbit head. Finally, I pulled it off my hand. But bits of fur and sticky melted flesh clung to my fingers.

I stared down at the waxy gray puddle on my table. A few seconds ago, that puddle had been Benny.

Swallowing hard, I took a step back. I realized the whole bedroom had become steamy hot. A hot white mist floated up from the floor. The window was completely fogged.

"Nicky? Tara? Are you here?" I called. "I . . . I need help!"

No answer.

The steamy mist filled my room. I heard a low hiss, which grew louder . . . louder . . . until it sounded like a wild rainstorm. I covered my ears, but I couldn't block out the shrill sound.

And then my mouth opened in a silent cry as I realized I was no longer alone.

A dark figure floated out of the fog—and I recognized him at once. Recognized his blond hair, his long dark overcoat. Recognized his cold blue eyes.

Mr. Morgo!

"How did you get in here?" I cried, my voice cracking. "What are you doing here?"

He smiled and didn't reply. The fog settled around him. I could see damp puddles on my carpet. Streams of water trailed down my wallpaper.

Morgo lowered his eyes to the melted rabbit on my table. "That's what I'm going to do to you," he said, "if you don't return what you stole."

My mouth dropped open. My breath caught in my throat. "S-stole?"

He nodded. He stepped forward, and I felt a wave of heat move against my body. Morgo stuck a gloved finger into the middle of the melted rabbit. At his touch, it sizzled and hissed.

"You know what I'm talking about," Morgo said softly.

"No," I said, my whole body trembling. "No, I don't."

"I'm not a patient man," Morgo said. He pointed his finger at me.

Another wave of heat washed over me. And then my face grew hot. I felt my ears start to burn. My earlobes were sticking to my face.

"No, please—!" I shouted. "Don't *melt* me!"

"Then return what you stole," Morgo said, lowering his gloved hand.

I rubbed my ears. They were still burning hot, but they hadn't melted.

"The life pods . . . ," Morgo said. "Return them to me—now."

"Life pods?" I gasped. "I—I didn't take any life pods."

"They're silver," Morgo replied through clenched teeth. "They're shaped like bullets."

My mouth dropped open. Those things were *life pods?*

"It isn't nice to steal," Morgo said, gazing at me with his cold eyes. "I let you and your friend enjoy my haunted house. I didn't expect you to steal valuable property. Now, give them back. Give them back *now!*"

I panicked. I didn't think. "But I don't have them!" I blurted out. "I gave them to Traci!"

I knew at once that I'd made a terrible mistake.

But who can think straight with an evil ghost in your bedroom about to melt you?

"I'll find this Traci," Morgo said, shoving his gloved hands into his overcoat pockets. "Time to find Traci."

What have I done?

I can't let him go after Traci.

74

"But . . . Traci can't see you!" I cried. "*I'm* the only one who can see and hear ghosts."

Morgo's smile turned into a sneer. "Don't worry. She'll know I'm there," he said. "It will be the *last* thing she ever knows!"

18

MR. MORGO FLOATED OUT the window. Before he left, he melted my clock radio. I stared at it, swallowing hard. I had a knot in my throat as big as a softball. Maybe it was my heart!

"Nicky? Tara? Please? I need help!"

No. No sign of my ghost friends.

I started to the door. Then I turned and came back. I paced back and forth for a few seconds. I glimpsed the melted rabbit and my whole body shuddered.

I'd never felt panic like this.

Was Morgo going to melt Traci?

No. I can't let him. It would be my fault! I knew I had to get to Traci first.

The phone! I grabbed my phone and punched in her number. "Traci—please be there!" I cried.

One ring. Two . . . three . . . four . . .

No. No answer. No one home.

I've got to find her. I've got to get those pendants back before . . . before Morgo does something horrible!

I pulled on my boots, grabbed my parka, and shot out of the house. A blast of cold wind felt good against my hot cheeks. The sky was solid gray, and the strong wind swept snow off the ground and sent it flying in all directions.

I ran into the middle of the street. The plow had come by, shoving snow to the curbs on both sides. It had made hills of snow nearly as tall as me.

Across the street, some little kids were building a snow fort. A car skidded in its driveway, tires whining on the ice. Mrs. Murray, our neighbor, drove by, moving slowly on the slippery road.

My breath puffed up in front of me as I trotted down Bleek Street. With the gray sky above me and the white snow all around, I suddenly felt as if I was running through an unreal world. A distant planet where everything was black and white. And cold . . . chillingly cold.

I was wishing I was somewhere else. Not running through my snowy neighborhood to Traci's house. Not running in terror from a ghost who could melt a cute bunny rabbit and not even care.

Running from a ghost who could melt a *human*.

I'll get those pendants back, I told myself.

Did Morgo call them *life pods*?

I'll get the pods back from Traci. I'll return

them to Morgo. And then in fifty or sixty years, I'll be able to forget how frightened I am right now!

That's what I was thinking when I saw a group of kids at the top of Miller Hill, a block from Traci's house. Some were pulling sleds. Others had plastic disks. Four or five kids were perched on the snow mountain made by the plows, tossing snowballs at kids across the street.

And was that blond girl in the red down jacket Traci? The one carrying the red snow disk?

Yes.

Traci! Thank goodness!

Gasping for breath, I ran as fast as I could, slipping and stumbling in the deep, slick snow. I reached the top of the hill just as Traci went sliding down.

Miller Hill is steep and a mile long. You just keep going down forever.

I watched Traci raise both hands in the air as her sled picked up speed. Her blond hair flew out from under her ski cap, and she screamed all the way to the bottom.

"Traci!" I shouted.

The snowball fight grew bigger. Kids were laughing and screaming. Two little boys went down the hill sharing a Flexible Flyer.

I cupped my hands and shouted again. "Traci! Up here! It's me! Traci—I need those metal things back!"

She didn't look up. She was talking to some girls at the bottom of the hill. They had to dodge out of the way as the two little boys came shooting down the hill.

"Traci—hi!" I screamed at the top of my lungs. "Traci—come up here!"

Finally, she heard me. She turned and shouted, "Stay away from me, Max. You're too weird!"

Oh, wow. She was still upset about the cookies and milk flying through the air.

How could I tell her she had a *lot more* to be upset about?

"Traci—I have to talk to you! I—I'm coming down!"

My shouts were cut off by a hard shove at my side. I spun around and saw the Wilbur brothers looming over me.

Willy had a pair of ice skates dangling around his neck. Billy dropped the plastic garbage bag he was using as a sled and shoved me again. "Get lost, Maxie. You're ruining our race."

"Huh? Race?" I sneered at him. "What race? You two aren't even in the *human* race."

Why do I always make bad jokes when I'm about to be pounded to a pulp?

"You're in the way," Billy said. He bumped me hard with his chest.

"Hey, give me a break just once," I pleaded. "This is important."

79

I turned and called to Traci again. But she was gone. She and the other girls had completely vanished. Did they go to Traci's house?

A loud hissing sound made me gasp. Morgo!

No. Just two cats chasing each other through the snow.

"You want a break? We'll give you a break, Maxie," Willy Wilbur said. He pulled back the collar of my coat. Billy scooped up a massive pile of snow—and dropped it down my back.

The two of them laughed and slapped high fives. They think they're riots.

I don't have time for this, I thought. Any second now, Traci will be a melted puddle, and it will be all my fault.

I turned and gazed down to the bottom of the hill. To my horror, I saw Traci walking away with two other girls.

"No! Come back! Traci—come back!" I screamed.

She didn't hear me.

Now what? Now what?

Suddenly, I had an idea.

19

THE DRIVEWAY TO TRACI'S house had been shoveled, but her mom's SUV still had snow on the roof and over the back window. I crouched behind it in the driveway and stared at the house.

The garage door was open. I could see her dad's Camry inside. Two cars here meant that her parents were probably home.

This made my job a lot tougher.

Were they in the front of the house or the back? I made my way along the side of the house to the kitchen. My heart began to thud in my chest. I'd never sneaked into anyone's house before.

A snowblower stood at the back of the house next to a shovel. I stepped around them and crept toward the kitchen window.

Anyone in there? The sun covered the window with yellow light. I couldn't see a thing.

I'll try the kitchen door, I thought. If I can get through the kitchen, it'll be an easy run to the front stairs, then up to Traci's room.

I heard the TV. Maybe the parents and her little brother were all in the den. I'd only been in Traci's house once, for a birthday party when we were five or six. But I remembered a wood-paneled den with a big TV at the back of the house.

I crossed my gloved fingers for luck.

Just let me grab those metal things and get out of here without being seen.

Taking a deep breath, I stepped up to the back stoop. My boot slipped on a patch of ice and I fell forward. My head banged the kitchen door.

I froze. Did anyone hear that? Was someone coming?

Hunched over, I waited, not moving or breathing. After a few seconds, I pulled myself up. Okay. No problem. Easy does it, here.

I reached for the doorknob—and the door swung open.

I gasped and staggered back. "Hi," I choked out. "I . . . I'm a friend of Traci's."

Mrs. Wayne gasped too. "I didn't see you back here. You startled me."

She wore a bulky red ski sweater over black leggings and had a red wool cap pulled down over her blond hair. She looked like Traci's twin, only older. She pulled a pair of skis out of the house.

"I'm meeting some friends," she said, stepping onto the stoop. "We're doing some cross-country."

She squinted at me. "What are you doing back here?"

"Uh . . . looking for Traci," I said. "I have to ask her something . . . about school."

Mrs. Wayne started toward her SUV. "Traci is at Miller Hill," she said. "Didn't you pass her? She's sledding with a whole bunch of kids from your class."

"Thanks," I said. "I'll go back and find her."

But I didn't do that. I headed to the sidewalk and trudged slowly toward Miller Hill. But as soon as Mrs. Wayne backed down the drive and pulled away, I turned and hurried back to the house.

Again I listened at the kitchen door. The TV was going in the den. I grabbed the knob, pushed open the door, and sneaked into the kitchen.

It was warm inside. The house smelled like hot chocolate. I saw three empty cups on the sink. I could hear the TV in the next room. A Sponge-Bob cartoon. Traci's little brother was probably in there. But where was her father?

I crept as silently as I could toward the front of the house. I saw that my boots were leaving dirty puddles of water on the kitchen floor. But what could I do?

I found the front stairs and started to climb. The wooden steps creaked beneath me. Could anyone hear? My skin tingled. I was alert to every sound.

I reached the top of the stairs. The hall lights were on. I saw four bedrooms, a bathroom, and some closets. If Mr. Wayne was up here, I'd be totally busted.

Holding my breath, I tiptoed down the hall. It didn't take long to find Traci's room. I crept inside and carefully closed the door behind me.

I glanced around as I waited to catch my breath. Traci had two framed posters of ballerinas on the wall over her bed. I kinda remembered she was into dance.

The room was a cluttered mess. Books and papers and CDs and DVDs tossed everywhere. A big brown basket on the floor overflowed with magazines.

The bed wasn't made. Dirty clothes were strewn over it. Stuffed animals, schoolbooks, backpacks, a boom box, jeans and T-shirts, empty shopping bags—all on the floor.

Wow. A whole new hidden *messy* side of Traci!

But where were the six life pods?

Her desk was just as messy as the rest of the room. The computer was on, a screen saver of fish floating across the monitor.

She had a photo of Buddy, her old dog, next to a photo of herself in a ballerina costume at age seven or so.

I pulled off my gloves and started pushing things around on her desk. I examined a big cup full of pens and pencils. I pulled open the desk drawers, all crammed with stuff, and poked through everything.

No. No sign of the pendants.

My legs trembled.

I jumped at every sound.

I knew that Morgo would come at any second. If I couldn't find the pendants and return them to him, he'd melt me—and Traci, too.

I moved to her makeup table, cluttered with bottles and tubes and soaps and eye pencils and sponges and stuff. But no pendants.

I was about to turn away when I glimpsed a red box on the corner of her dresser. A jewelry box. Yes! She must have dropped the six pendants into her jewelry box.

They *had* to be here. I started toward the dresser. A loud creak made me stop. Morgo?

I spun to the windows. No. Not here—yet.

I grabbed Traci's jewelry box and lifted the top. Tiny earrings and a couple of silver chains. No. No pendants.

I lifted the top shelf of the jewelry box to look underneath.

And the bedroom door swung open.

"Oh!" I cried out. And dropped the shelf of earrings as Traci strode into the room.

"Max? Are you crazy?" she cried. "What are you doing in my room?"

20

"T-Traci—" I sputtered. "I—"

"How did you get up here?" she demanded. She had her parka on. Her cheeks were still red from the cold. Her hands were balled into tight fists. "Why are you going through my stuff?"

I was desperate to explain, but my tongue suddenly stuck to the roof of my mouth. The only sound I could make was "Hmmmmma hmm-mma."

Traci pulled off her parka and tossed it onto the floor. "I don't get it," she said, frowning at me. "Did my parents let you up here? Or did you sneak into my house?"

"I snuck in," I said. I could finally talk. "Traci, it . . . it's hard to explain. But I need those silver pendants back. Right away."

"I gave them to Phoebe Mullin," she said. "We're working together on the necklace."

My mouth dropped open. "Phoebe has them?"

She nodded. "You can't take them back. We need them."

"You—you don't understand!" I stammered. "They're dangerous!"

I couldn't tell her the truth. I couldn't tell her that Morgo, a vicious ghost, was probably melting Phoebe into a puddle of wax right now.

"What's wrong with them?" Traci demanded. "What's so dangerous, Max?"

I didn't answer. I slid past her and took off. I bolted down the stairs and out the front door. I could hear Traci's dad shouting behind me, "Who's there?" But I couldn't stop to answer.

It's all my fault.

That's what I kept repeating in my mind.

Phoebe has probably been melted—*and it's all my fault!*

My boots crunched over the snow as I started to run. I had been to Phoebe's house before. It was three or four blocks away. I knew I had to get there as fast as I could.

I was nearly at the curb when two figures stepped out from behind a tree. They jumped in front of me and grabbed me by the sleeves of my parka.

The Wilbur brothers!

"No time!" I gasped.

"What's up, Maxie?" Willy asked.

"How's it going?" Billy asked.

"Let go," I said breathlessly. "I—I have to

hurry." I twisted hard, trying to free myself. But those two guys are *big*—and totally strong.

"No snowmen around to help you this time," Willy Wilbur said, glancing around the block. "But you're really into snowmen, right?"

"No. No way," I said. "Give me a break, guys. I really am in a hurry. I—"

They picked me up and heaved me into a tall snowdrift. Then they held me down and began piling snow over me.

"Let me up!" I tried to scramble to my feet. But I was buried in the high drift. And they were packing it tighter, making it impossible to escape.

"See? Max is really into snow," Billy said.

"He's really *into* it," Willy said.

That made them both giggle like idiots.

How funny are they? *Not!*

Icy snow pressed against my face. I struggled to breathe. My teeth started to chatter.

Silence now. I waited and listened. Did they leave?

Lying on my back, I swung my shoulder hard, pushing snow away. The cold froze my cheeks. Icy snow dripped down my neck. I swung my shoulder again, making a little more room. Then I twisted my body—pushed and squirmed and twisted—until I was lying on my stomach.

I lowered my hands to the bottom of the snow and pushed up. Yes! Straining every muscle, I hoisted myself up . . . and out of the snowdrift. My mouth fell open and I gasped for air, sucking in deep cold breaths.

My whole body shook. My jeans were soaked. My parka felt wet and stiff.

With a groan, I freed one leg, then the other, and stepped out of the drift. I shook myself hard, like a dog, sending snow spraying all around me.

Okay. Thank you, Wilbur brothers, for that special treat.

They thought they had played a funny joke on poor Max. They had no way of knowing they could have cost Phoebe Mullin her life.

I pictured her copper-colored ponytail, her freckled face, her red and blue braces that showed when she smiled, the yellow T-shirt she wore that said BOYS STINK in big black letters.

I remembered her swinging in a tire in her backyard. It was some kind of party, and we all climbed on with her and acted like chimpanzees, scratching and grunting and—

Whoa, Max. Get it together, dude.

I shook myself hard again, shaking away the memories. And I started to run over the snow. Shivering, my teeth chattering, I ran in a total panic. The houses, the trees and bushes, the cars that rolled by—I didn't see any of them. I saw the white snow ahead of me, my breath puffing up against the sky, and a blur of colors and sounds.

By the time I reached Phoebe's block, I was panting hard, my chest aching. My nose and ears were frozen numb, and my cheeks burned from the cold.

Did I get to Phoebe before Morgo?

I stopped across the street from Phoebe's house. Blinked once. Blinked twice.

And stared at the pile of blue trash in the driveway. Why would Phoebe's parents leave that in front of the house?

I crossed the street, and it came into clearer focus. I saw part of a shiny bumper . . . a bent and twisted license plate.

"Oh nooooo." A low wail escaped my throat.

It wasn't a pile of trash. It was the Mullins' car. Melted in the driveway.

Was Phoebe inside it?

21

FRANTICALLY, I TRIED TO search for Phoebe inside the car. But it was a big solid puddle—there *was* no inside!

Heart pounding, I spun away from it, ran up the walk—and burst into the house. I didn't even ring the bell.

"Who's there?" Mr. Mullin jumped up from his armchair in the den. His newspaper fell out of his hands.

He is tall and very thin, with a face like a field mouse—long nose and tiny gray eyes that always look as if they're squinting. "What on earth—?" he cried.

"Sorry to break in," I said breathlessly, gazing around. "Where's Phoebe?"

"She's gone," he said. "I don't understand—"

"Gone? What do you mean *gone*?" I cried.

"Gone to school. She's rehearsing a play." He bent to pick up his newspaper. "You're Max Doyle, right? Listen, Max, you can't just barge into someone's house and—"

"Can I search her room?" I asked.

He narrowed his little gray eyes at me again. "Excuse me? Search her room? Of course not. Are you crazy?"

"No, I'm not crazy. But I can't explain," I said. "Does Phoebe have a bunch of pendants that look like this?" I reached under my sweatshirt, pulled off the silver pendant I always wear, and handed it to Mr. Mullin.

He held it away from him, as if I'd just handed him a bomb. "How should I know, Max? I don't keep track of her jewelry."

I glanced around the room in a panic. What should I do? Morgo had definitely been here. Did Morgo find the pendants in Phoebe's room? Or did Phoebe take them to school with her? I had to find out.

"Does she have a cell phone?" I asked Mr. Mullin. "I really have to talk to her."

He stood tensely, newspaper in one hand, frowning at me. "No. No cell phone." He pointed to the front door. "Maybe you could come back, Max. Why don't you come back later? I'm going to pick her up in an hour."

"Pick her up?" I cried. "Have you *looked* at your car?"

"My car? What about my car?"

I guess he hadn't looked out the front window. *No way* did I want to stay around and explain. "Sorry to bother you," I said, and I took off.

I had to run to school and hope to get to Phoebe in time. The melted blue car in the Mullins' driveway made my stomach churn.

I'd never run so much in my life. My legs ached—everything ached—and my cold, wet clothes stuck to my skin.

Slipping and sliding, I turned onto Powell Avenue and continued to jog. Finally, the school came into view.

At the top of the flagpole, the flag flapped hard in the wind. Jefferson Elementary is a kind of old-fashioned-looking three-story brick building.

Snow clung to the roof, and long, fat icicles dripped down from the gutters. Someone had tossed snowballs at the front wall, which was dotted with circles of snow.

I took a deep breath, started to run up the front walk—and stopped.

I stared at the narrow path beside the front walk. A trail of melted snow. The snow had melted completely away, and the green grass showed.

Melted snow . . . and the path led right to the front door of the school.

Morgo was here!

Oh no. Poor Phoebe.

I pulled open the front door and slipped inside.

My legs trembled as I made my way down the long hall to the auditorium. My mouth suddenly felt so dry, I couldn't swallow. I could barely breathe.

Morgo was here. Morgo got here first.

I turned the corner and stopped. Oh no . . . oh no. Heaped on the floor at the end of the hall—a dark melted puddle.

Phoebe?

22

I FROZE.

I stared down the hall at the dark mound spread over the floor. I started to shiver and I couldn't stop.

Finally, gritting my teeth, I forced myself to move. I staggered down the hall. Trembling, I stepped close to the puddle.

"Phoebe?" The name burst from my lips.

But no. The dark heap came into focus. A coat. Someone's winter coat tossed onto the floor.

I opened my mouth and started to laugh. I couldn't help it. I felt so relieved.

But I cut my celebration short. Mr. Morgo was here. Phoebe was in major danger.

I stepped around the coat and pushed open the doors to the auditorium. I heard voices on the stage.

As I made my way down the aisle, I saw Mrs. Manola, the drama teacher. She was talking to a bunch of kids in a circle around her. They all stood in front of a painted backdrop of big-city skyscrapers.

My eyes followed the circle, and I saw Phoebe near the front. She wore a baggy blue sweater over dark straight-legged jeans.

Running to the stage, I opened my mouth to call to her. But two kids suddenly appeared in front of me, blocking my path.

Nicky and Tara!

"What are *you* doing here?" I cried.

Mrs. Manola turned and looked down from the stage. "We're rehearsing a play, Max," she said.

The kids all turned and stared at me.

"Maxie, we need to talk to you," Tara said, pulling my parka sleeve.

"You shouldn't be here!" I told her.

The kids onstage laughed. Mrs. Manola narrowed her eyes at me. "We shouldn't be? Well, what are *you* doing here, Max?"

"We're going to Doom House," Tara said.

"Don't go there!" I said.

The kids laughed again.

Mrs. Manola walked to the edge of the stage and peered down at me. "I have to ask you to leave, Max."

I turned to Nicky and Tara. "Can't you see I'm busy now?"

Mrs. Manola's expression turned angry. "*We're* the ones who are busy. You're interrupting our play rehearsal. Please leave, Max."

"Listen to me. We have to go to Doom House,"

Nicky said. "If the ghosts there are real, maybe they can help us find our parents."

"No. It's too dangerous," I said.

Mrs. Manola frowned at me. "Too dangerous to leave the auditorium?"

"We have to take the chance," Nicky said. "We're going there. We're desperate."

"Max, you don't belong here. I'm asking you politely to leave," Mrs. Manola said.

"Please don't go there!" I said.

Nicky and Tara waved good-bye and vanished.

It took me a few seconds to realize the kids on the stage were all laughing at me.

"Max, you're being very rude," Mrs. Manola said.

"I'm sorry. I wasn't talking to you," I said.

She glanced around the auditorium. "Well, who were you talking to? Ghosts?"

Big laughter onstage.

"Well . . . actually . . . ," I started. But I realized I didn't have time to waste. I turned away from Mrs. Manola. "Phoebe, I have to talk to you."

Phoebe let out a cry of surprise. "Me?"

I started to call her down to the auditorium floor. But a loud sizzling sound made me stop.

A wave of heat rolled over me, hot enough to make my skin prickle. "Whoa." I unzipped my parka.

"It's getting very hot in here," Mrs. Manola said, shaking her head. She stared at the radiator. "Where is all that heat coming from?"

Kids started to groan and complain as the temperature rose. Sweat poured down their faces. Behind them, I saw the painted backdrop start to droop.

"The furnace must be going berserk," Mrs. Manola said, fanning herself with her clipboard.

But I knew differently.

I felt another blast of heat on my back. I spun around and saw Mr. Morgo standing behind me. He had a strange tight smile on his face.

"Mr. Morgo—please!" I cried. But he ignored me. He walked right through me, and my body heaved as if on fire.

I knew I was the only one who could see him. But what could I do? I watched helplessly as he floated up to the stage.

"I'm tired of racing around from place to place," he said. "I've been following you, Max. I knew you'd lead me to the stolen life pods. But I'm sick of searching."

Only I heard him.

And only I saw him raise both hands and point them toward the kids onstage.

And only I knew what he planned to do—melt everyone in sight.

23

"MORGO—STOP!" I SHOUTED.

Kids stared down at me.

"Max, who are you talking to?" Mrs. Manola demanded. Her hair drooped wetly over her face. The front of her turtleneck sweater was stained with sweat.

Several kids dropped to their knees, unable to stand the burning heat. But the stage floor was hot, and they jumped right back up.

Steam hissed on the stage and out over the rows of seats.

Morgo held his hands high. His features were set in an angry scowl. He waved his right hand— and the backdrop started to melt.

Kids screamed and scampered away from it.

The skyscrapers appeared to fold. The backdrop curled wetly to the stage floor.

"What is *happening*?" Mrs. Manola screamed. "We'd better leave, people. Use the stage door."

"Don't let them leave!" Morgo shouted at me.

At the back of the stage, Mrs. Manola grabbed

the doorknob at the exit. She let out a high shriek and jumped back. She shook her hand hard, blowing on it.

"Don't touch that knob!" she cried to the others. "It's . . . burning hot!"

Morgo turned to me. "I want those life pods—now," he said through clenched teeth. "I don't want to melt your friends, Max."

"Uh . . . it would be really great if you didn't melt them," I said. "I mean, I'm sure everyone would be really happy not to be melted."

"Shut up," Morgo said, shaking his head.

"Oh. Okay. No problem. Really."

"Shut up and find out who has the stolen pods," Morgo said. He swung his hand and three folding chairs on the stage melted into dark brown puddles.

Kids screamed. Mrs. Manola had her arms crossed tightly in front of her, as if trying to shield herself.

"Phoebe, I need your help!" I shouted.

Phoebe stared suspiciously at me. "What do you want?"

"You know those metal pendant things that Traci gave you?" I asked. "Do you have them? Could you give them to me?"

Phoebe wiped sweat from her forehead. "No, I couldn't use them, Max. I don't have them."

I saw Morgo tense his hands, preparing to melt everyone.

I turned back to Phoebe. "Well, where are they?" I shouted up to her.

"I returned them to *your* house," she said.

24

PHOEBE MUST HAVE RETURNED them on her way to the play rehearsal at school—while I was searching Traci's house.

Now what?

I didn't have long to think about it. Morgo floated off the stage and landed behind me. He grabbed my right arm and twisted it behind my back.

"Ow!" I let out a cry as his touch burned right through my parka sleeve.

Kids onstage were staring at me in disbelief. Why was I twisting my own arm back?

"Let's go, Max," Morgo said. He gave me a hard shove that sent me staggering. Then he pushed me up the aisle toward the exit.

Kids were shouting and laughing. I guess some of them thought I was clowning around.

But it was no joke.

Morgo held on to me all the way to my house. As we walked, we burned a path in the snow. People in cars stopped to stare at me.

"I want those life pods," Morgo said as we turned onto Bleek Street.

He pushed me toward the two snowmen on the curb. They both melted as we walked past.

"I . . . I've been trying to get them back for you all morning," I stammered. "Really. I don't want them. You can have them."

My skin throbbed and burned, as if I had a really bad sunburn. We melted a path in the snow up my driveway and to the back of the house.

Please don't melt me, I thought. I'll give you back your pods.

But please don't melt me.

I stamped the snow off my boots and pushed open the kitchen door. Was anyone home?

The house was silent.

I walked into the kitchen and started to pull off my wet boots.

"No time for that," Morgo said. He gave me another hard shove. His touch made the back of my parka sizzle. "Where are the pods?"

I searched the living room quickly, but I didn't see them. "Mom probably took them up to my room," I said.

I led the way upstairs. My heart was thudding like a bass drum. My legs suddenly felt rubbery and weak.

What if Colin was home? What if Phoebe

gave the pods to Colin and he threw them out? What would Morgo do if the pods weren't here?

I ran into my room and glanced all around. Not on the bed. Not on the chair. Not on the bed table.

"Yes!" I cried out when I saw the six silver pods on my desk next to the computer. "Yes! They're right here."

I scooped them into my hands and handed them to Morgo. "Here. Take them."

He stared at them, his lips moving as he counted them.

"They're all there," I said happily. "The life pods. All six of them."

Morgo raised his eyes to me. "So they are," he said softly. "So they are."

"Well . . . uh . . . good-bye," I said. I waved.

"Not so fast," Morgo said. "Now I'm going to punish you for being a thief."

"No, wait," I pleaded, staggering back as Morgo came toward me. "I'm not a thief. Really. I mean, yes, I did take those things. But that doesn't mean—"

Morgo raised his right hand and I felt a blast of heat sweep over me.

"Please don't melt me!" I screamed. "Please!"

A cold smile crossed Morgo's face. "I'm going to enjoy this," he whispered.

25

THE ROOM GREW HOT and wet. I saw the windows steam up.

I shut my eyes. And waited for the pain.

Then I heard the thud of footsteps.

I opened my eyes and saw Colin burst into the room. "Think fast!" he shouted.

He heaved a snowball at me. It hit me in the chest and splattered.

Snow sprayed onto Morgo's face. He let out a startled cry. Morgo turned and sent a wave of heat shooting over Colin.

My brother's eyes bulged wide in surprise. His hands shot out. His clothes started to melt.

Morgo frantically brushed snow off his forehead. His face twisted in pain.

He narrowed his eyes at me, gave me an icy stare—and vanished in a puff of white steam.

I turned back to Colin. He stood there quivering in shock—and totally naked! His melted clothes were a red and blue puddle around his bare feet.

"Max—you creep!" he shouted, shaking his fist at me. "How did you do that?"

"Uh . . . one of my new magic tricks," I said. "I'm still working on it."

Colin flashed me one more horrified look. Then he whirled around and ran to his room.

The room quickly cooled off. I took a few deep breaths. My heartbeat started to return to normal.

Mr. Morgo was gone. He had his precious life pods. Did that mean I was safe? Or would he come back to punish me for taking them?

Maybe I was okay for now. But I knew Nicky and Tara weren't.

I knew that Doom House wasn't safe. It wasn't a fake haunted house. Those ghosts were real. They had to be the ghosts that Phears had helped to escape.

Morgo seemed to be their new leader. And let's not kid around—he was evil. The other ghosts were evil too. *No way* would they help Nicky and Tara.

My two friends were walking into a trap.

Could I rescue them from that haunted house? I knew I had to try.

I still had my parka and boots on. I clumped into the hall. I could hear Colin in his room, slamming his dresser drawers, getting dressed again.

I made my way down the steps and headed to the front door. Before I could open the door, Mom jumped in front of me.

"Sorry, Maxie," she said, shaking her head. "You can't go outside. It isn't safe."

26

"**TAKE OFF YOUR COAT,**" Mom said. "It isn't safe out there."

"Not safe? Mom, what are you talking about?"

"I just talked to Mr. Mullin," she said. "His car melted. Right in the driveway. It just melted."

So what *else* is new?

"Things are melting all over the neighborhood," Mom said. "People think it's sunspots."

Sunspots? *You're kidding!*

"Mom—look outside," I said. "It's cloudy now. There won't be any sunspots."

She shook her head and pressed her back against the door. "No. You're not going outside until they say it's okay on TV."

"Mom, I really have to go. Some friends of mine are waiting for me and—"

She crossed her tiny arms in front of her. She shook her head again. "No way."

I tried to stare her down. But she wouldn't blink.

I sighed. "Okay. But this is stupid," I said. I turned and stomped back upstairs to my room.

I didn't take off my parka or boots. I started to pace back and forth, curling my hands into fists. Nicky and Tara needed me. Every second counted.

After a minute or two, I stepped to my bedroom door. I could hear Mom in the kitchen, humming to herself as she started to make dinner. My chance to escape.

Sorry, Mom. I'll watch out for sunspots.

I crept down the stairs, bolted out the front door, and closed it silently behind me.

The sun was going down. The sky was a deep purple. The gusting wind made the snow swirl around me.

I lowered my head against the wind and ran to the bus stop on Powell Avenue. I just missed a bus. I watched it rumble off down the next block. I stood there shivering, waiting for the next one.

Twenty minutes later, the next bus rolled up. I swiped my bus card through the fare machine and took a seat in the back. I was the only passenger.

By the time I reached Doom House on the other side of town, the sky was solid black. Low-hanging clouds covered the moon and stars.

No streetlights here. And no lights in the windows of the old mansion. The scrape of my boots as I made my way up the long driveway was the only sound I heard, except for the whistle of the wind through the quivering bare trees.

No sign of Mr. Morgo, at least. But what would I find inside? Were Nicky and Tara still here?

I slipped on a patch of ice. Caught my balance. Then, breathing hard, crunched my way along the side of the house.

Squinting in the darkness, I saw a low window near the back. The glass had been broken out. I stopped when I heard voices inside.

My heart started to pound. Sliding my boots over the snow, trying not to make a sound, I crept up to the window. Moving slowly, carefully, I peeked into the house—and let out a gasp of horror.

Ghosts—at least a dozen of them.

I saw a young boy with his eyes missing and a gaping hole where his nose should be. His lips flapped as he made a crazy jabbering sound.

He floated beside an old woman in a long, tattered gray dress. She was bald—and I saw long brown worms crawling over her scalp in place of hair.

One ghost had his head tossed back. His face was rutted with deep red scars. His yellow eyes rolled wildly as he stared at the ceiling, and he laughed at the top of his lungs, laughed without stopping.

Two young girl ghosts floated beside him. They

had clumps of dirt clinging to their clothes. When they raised their arms, I saw that the skin had rotted off their hands. Their bony fingers cracked loudly as they balled them into fists.

And in the middle of these ugly ghosts . . . trapped in the middle . . . I saw my two frightened friends, Nicky and Tara.

27

TARA GRIPPED NICKY'S ARM tightly. They both were trembling with fright. The ugly ghosts floated in a line now, laughing and hissing, whispering and jabbering. They backed Nicky and Tara up against a wall.

Flickering candles provided the only light. As I stared through the window, the ghosts appeared to fade in and out of the dancing shadows.

A tall, frail-looking ghost in overalls and a torn flannel shirt scratched his peeling scalp. His eyes glowed red in the candlelight, and he gave Nicky and Tara a cold, toothless smile.

Another ghost had half his face missing, the skull poking through on his left side.

I leaned on the windowsill and stared in through the broken window. I saw two bearded, scarred, scowling ghosts hold up two silver life pods.

Nicky and Tara glanced frantically around the room. I knew they were searching for a way to escape. But they were backed against the wall, and the ghosts pressed closer and closer.

"We'll keep you two inside these life pods for a while," a deep voice said.

And then I saw Mr. Morgo appear in the middle of the line of ghosts. His dark coat swirled around him. His hat was pulled low over his blond hair.

The bearded ghosts raised the life pods out toward Nicky and Tara.

"Let us go!" Tara cried in a high, trembling voice. "We can't help you."

"We're telling the truth!" Nicky shouted.

Morgo shook his head. "You'll be very comfortable inside a pod. Your parents kept *us* inside them—until Phears came along and stole the pods and set us all free."

He floated closer to Nicky and Tara. "Have you had the pleasure of meeting Phears?"

Nicky and Tara didn't answer. They both stared in horror at the life pods, shimmering in the flickering light.

"Why not make it easy on yourselves?" Morgo said. "Tell us where your parents are, and we'll let you go."

"We *told* you!" Tara cried. "We don't know. I swear!"

"We came here to ask you," Nicky added. "We hoped that *you* could help us find them."

The ghosts all laughed—chilling hoarse laughs that sounded like coughing.

Morgo was the only one who didn't laugh. He kept his icy blue-eyed stare on my two friends. "Well, why don't we just keep you snug and safe in one of these pods," he said. "And we'll all wait for your parents to come looking for you."

"No, please—" Tara begged.

"We can't help you. Really," Nicky said. "Don't make us go inside those things."

Morgo didn't reply. He nodded to one of the bearded ghosts. The ghost pointed his pod at Nicky and Tara.

I watched in horror as my two friends floated up off the floor. They both screamed. They were being sucked into the life pod.

They thrashed their arms and tried to twist their bodies free. But the force of the pod seemed too powerful.

Nicky and Tara screamed again, more faintly this time. They started to shrink. The pod pulled Nicky closer. His head was about to disappear into the silvery pod.

I gripped the windowsill. I knew I had to do something.

But what?

Could I distract the ghosts? Give Nicky and Tara just enough time to escape?

I had to try.

Holding on to the sill, I started to pull myself through the open window.

But before I could move, I felt a sharp stab of pain in my back. I'm hit, I thought. The ghosts got me. I'm hit. . . .

I let out a startled gasp—and slid to my knees in the snow.

28

I HEARD LAUGHTER BEHIND me.

The pain faded quickly. I spun around—and saw the Wilbur brothers' grinning faces. Billy and Willy came running across the snow, heaving snowballs at me.

The snowballs were hardpacked and icy. A sharp one had hit me in the back.

"I don't have time for this!" I shouted.

Inside the house, my friends were in terrible trouble. I didn't have time to waste on a snowball fight with the Wilburs.

"Go away! Get away!" I screamed.

Furious, I picked up one of their ice balls and heaved it back at them. Billy ducked and it sailed over his head.

He pulled back his arm, launched a big snowball at me—and it flew through the open window of the house.

A shrill scream burst out the window. A ghostly wail.

The Wilbur brothers dropped their snowballs.

Their eyes bulged in fright. "Who screamed?" Willy asked. They both stared at the house.

Another long, loud howl of pain floated from inside.

"I'm outta here!" Billy cried.

Slipping on the snow, the two Wilburs took off running. Willy's cap blew off his head, and he didn't stop to pick it up.

I watched them disappear through the scraggly hedges at the front of the yard. Then I turned to the window and peered inside.

To my surprise, one of the bearded ghosts was doubled over in pain. I watched him frantically brushing snow off his chest.

The other ghosts were frozen in place, watching the bearded ghost's struggle. Nicky and Tara backed themselves against the wall.

What happened here? I asked myself.

What happened?

And suddenly, it became clear.

I spotted a snow shovel leaning against the side of the house. I ran over to it, grabbed it, and hurried back to the window.

Bending low, I plunged the shovel into the deep snow and filled it. Then, using all my strength, I heaved a huge pile of snow high into the window.

I heard cries and screams. Howls of pain.

But I didn't stop to see what was going on in there. I dug the blade in again, deep into the snow—and swung another shovelful into the room. Then another. Another. Not stopping to take a breath. Making the snow fly fast and hard.

More screams rang out. Shrill wails of pain and terror. And then the screams were drowned out by a sizzling hiss. It reminded me of fried eggs and bacon crackling on the stove.

As I heaved in shovel after shovel, I remembered Tara's pain when she was hit by snow. Remembered how it had burned her. And I remembered how the snow had burned Morgo, too.

And I remembered the words that Lulu had murmured to Nicky and Tara: *"Colder than the grave."*

That's what it would take to defeat these ghosts. Something colder than the grave. Like *snow!*

Yes! I listened to the sizzling hiss. The sound of ghosts burning, burning in pain. And knew I had melted them all, melted them with something *colder than the grave.*

My arms ached. Sweat poured down my face.

Silence now. The sizzling had stopped. No more ghostly howls and screams of pain.

I lowered my hands to my knees and struggled to catch my breath. My gloves were soaked. My chest ached.

I grabbed the windowsill and hoisted myself up. I squinted into the flickering candlelight.

No one in there. No sign of the ghosts. Except for the two silvery life pods on the floor.

"Hey—anyone still here?" I shouted in.

No reply.

I'd done it. I'd destroyed the ghosts. But . . . wait!

"Oh noooo!" I let out a horrified moan.

The evil ghosts were all gone. *But so were Nicky and Tara!*

29

A HEAVY FEELING OF dread slid over me. I stared into the empty room, watching the shadows dart and dance.

Only shadows. No one left.

"Nicky? Tara?" I called their names. "Are you here? Please—be here!"

No reply.

I sighed and tried again, shouting their names. But no. They weren't here.

Why hadn't I looked? I'd heaved all that snow into the room without aiming it. Without thinking. I'd destroyed the evil ghosts—and my friends along with them.

With another long, sad sigh, I lowered myself into the house. The room smelled smoky. It smelled like our kitchen after Mom burned the roast.

I spun around, searching for any clue that Nicky and Tara might still be here, any clue that they might be okay.

My boots bumped one of the life pods on the floor.

Yes! The life pods!

Excited, I grabbed them both up and lifted them close to my face.

"Nicky? Tara? Are you in there?" I shouted at the top of my lungs into the pods.

Silence.

I carried the pods over to a candle and examined them in the light. I turned them over and over in my hands. I shouted my friends' names again.

No. Nicky and Tara weren't trapped inside.

With an angry cry, I tossed the two pods to the floor. They hit hard and bounced away.

Nicky and Tara were my best friends, I realized. They tried to help me in school. They tried to make me a braver, more popular person.

Yes, my best friends . . .

They had come to me for help. They were frightened and alone, and they'd asked me to help them find their parents.

And what did I do?

I *murdered* them. I murdered my best friends.

Furious, I kicked a pod against the wall. Then I dragged myself to the window, climbed back out into the wind and the blowing snow. And I trudged, head down, to the bus stop.

I rode the bus to Powell Avenue. I was so unhappy, so lost in my thoughts about Nicky and Tara, I almost missed my stop.

The heavy clouds had rolled away. A yellow full moon shone down, making the snow gleam like gold.

I started to pass Traci Wayne's house when I saw her in the front yard. All the tree lights were on, making her yard nearly as bright as day.

Traci waved to me. She had a bunch of friends with her. "Hey, Max," she called. "We're building a snow house. Want to help us?"

Huh? Traci Wayne was inviting me over? Inviting me to join her friends?

Normally, I'd go nuts, maybe do a few cartwheels, scream and beat my chest like a gorilla.

"No thanks," I called.

You don't murder your friends and then go build a snow house—even if your friends were ghosts.

I lowered my head and kept walking. Crossing the street, I stepped into a deep snowdrift, and icy snow poured into my boot. I hardly noticed.

All the lights were on in my house. I knew Mom would be angry because I sneaked out when she'd told me to stay inside.

I sure didn't feel like eating anything. My stomach was knotted and heavy as a rock.

I knew my family would be in the kitchen. So I sneaked in the front door and crept silently upstairs to my room. I didn't want to see anyone. I closed the door behind me and locked it. Then I clicked on the light.

Blinking, I waited for my eyes to adjust to the brightness. Then I turned to the bed—and let out a cry.

"What are *you* doing here?"

30

I STARED AT NICKY and Tara, sitting side by side on my bed. They both smiled at me. "What's up, Max?" Nicky said.

"You—you're *alive*!" I screamed. "You're okay! You—you—you—" I couldn't get the words out. I was so happy, so thrilled to see them.

They leaped off the bed and we all jumped up and down. And then we ran around in circles and did a crazy dance and then jumped up and down again.

Finally, we collapsed to the floor, gasping for breath. "You're alive! The ghosts are dead, and you're alive!" I cried.

"Well . . . we're not exactly *alive*," Tara said.

"But we're still here, thanks to you," Nicky said, slapping me a high five.

"We got out of there as soon as the snow started to fly," Tara said. "We knew it would be a massacre. We ran like crazy!"

"How did you figure it out, Max?" Nicky asked. "I guess they don't call you Brainimon for nothing!"

We slapped some more high fives. I was starting to come out of my shock.

"I . . . I almost *killed* you," I said, shaking my head.

"Hey, no problem," Nicky said. "It turned out okay—right?"

"And we learned a lot," Tara said. "Those silver pods. Our parents used them to imprison ghosts."

"Yeah. Ghosts can shrink and live inside those things," Nicky said. "Mom and Dad used them to hold the evil ghosts prisoner."

"They almost put *us* in one," Tara said. And then her mouth dropped open. "Hey!"

Suddenly, Nicky and Tara were both staring hard at me.

"Max, the pod you wear around your neck," Tara said. "Your mother gave it to you—right?"

I nodded. "Yeah. She found it on the floor the day we moved into this house. She put it on a chain and gave it to me for good luck."

Tara grabbed my arm. Her eyes were wide with excitement. "Don't you see? The pod was in this house—by itself. Not with the others. Maybe Mom and Dad are inside it. Maybe we've *found* them!" Her voice broke.

"You're wearing the pod," Nicky said. "Maybe that's the reason *you're* the only one who can see and hear us."

"Let's see it, Max," Tara cried. "Let's check it out!"

Both ghosts were bursting with excitement.

"Oh, I hope, I hope we're right!" Tara cried, crossing her fingers and hopping up and down. "Hurry, Max!"

I felt pretty excited too. I reached under my sweatshirt for the pendant.

"Oh, wow!" I cried. "It . . . it's *gone!*"

TO BE CONTINUED

ABOUT THE AUTHOR

Robert Lawrence Stine's scary stories have made him one of the bestselling children's authors in history. "Kids like to be scared!" he says, and he has proved it by selling more than 300 million books. R.L. teamed up with Parachute Press to create Fear Street, the first and number one bestselling young adult horror series. He then went on to launch Goosebumps, the creepy bestselling series that gave kids chills all over the world and made him the number one children's author of all time (*The Guinness Book of Records*).

R.L. Stine lives in Manhattan with his wife, Jane, their son, Matthew, and their dog, Nadine. He says he has never seen a ghost—but he's still looking!

Check out this sneak preview of the fourth book
in R.L. Stine's Mostly Ghostly:

Little Camp of Horrors

THIS SUMMER MAX IS going to Camp Snake
Lake—where he will have to swim in a lake filled
with poisonous snakes . . .
where a Headless Ghost roams the fields . . .
where he and his mostly ghostly friends, Nicky
and Tara, will continue the dangerous search for
Nicky and Tara's parents.

But first Max will have to face the evil spirit
Phears again. Can Max learn the secret that will
destroy this most terrifying ghoul for good?

MOM STEPPED OVER THE clutter on the floor. "Max, please change your mind," she said. "Go to summer camp with Colin. He's leaving in a few minutes on the counselors' bus with the other junior counselors. Let me pack you up."

"No way," I said, crossing my arms over my chest. "I told you. I'm allergic to trees. I can't help it. Even if I see a tree in a movie, I break out in spots."

"That can't be true," Colin said, bursting into my room. "Because you were *born* in a tree!"

Dad came in right behind him. He laughed at Colin's stupid joke.

"At least I was born, not dredged from a swamp," I said to Colin.

No one laughed at that.

No one ever laughs at my jokes.

Mom brushed a hand through my hair. "You don't have to go with Colin. You can take the camp bus tomorrow with the regular campers."

"Forget it," I muttered. "I can't go to camp. Fresh air makes me cough."

Dad shook his head and scowled at me. "How do you plan to spend your summer, Max? Doing stupid card tricks in your bedroom?"

I picked up a deck of cards from my bed table. "Here. Pick a card, any card."

Colin grabbed a puzzle magazine and flipped through it. "Check this out. *One Hundred and One Anagrams*. And he's worked them all."

He pinched my cheek really hard. "Like to waste time, Maxie?"

I grabbed the magazine out of his hand. "Know what an anagram of *Colin* is?" I asked. "It's *stupid*."

"Please don't fight," Mom said. She said that at least a hundred times a day. Mom is tiny like a little bird, with a quiet little voice, and she doesn't like yelling.

Dad took the deck of cards from me. "You have to get over your fears, Max," he said. "Summer camp will help you."

"I'm not afraid," I replied. "I just don't want to go!"

"Colin will be there to protect you," Mom said.

"Yeah, you got that right." Colin grinned at me. "Know what I'll protect you from? I'll protect you from gut punches. Like this!"

He punched me so hard in the stomach, I thought his hand went out my back! I doubled over, holding my aching gut, groaning like a dying seal.

Mom hurried over to me. "Colin, why did you do that to Maxie?" she asked.

Colin grinned again. "For fun?"

"Unnnnk unnnk," I moaned.

Colin turned to Dad. "I know why Max won't come to my camp. He's afraid he might have to swim in Snake Lake. I told him how it's filled with deadly poisonous snakes."

"That would toughen him up," Dad said.

"No one has ever come out of Snake Lake alive," Colin said, lowering his voice and trying to sound scary.

I shuddered. I guess he *did* sound scary.

"And get this," Colin said to Dad. "When I told Max the story of the Headless Camper, he almost wet his pants."

Dad and Colin both hee-hawed.

"You're a liar!" I cried.

"Stop scaring Maxie with those awful camp stories," Mom scolded.

"It doesn't matter," I said. "I'm not going. No way."

We heard a horn honk out on the street.

"The bus!" Colin cried. "It's here!"

Dad and I grabbed Colin's bags. Then we all

hurried downstairs to load him onto the bus. I suddenly felt very happy. A whole summer without Colin! Now, *that's* a vacation!

The bus driver came out to help with the bags. Inside the small yellow school bus, three or four other guys about Colin's age stared out at us. The bus said CAMP NAKE AKE on the side. Someone had pulled off some of the letters.

Mom hugged Colin. Dad hugged him too. Then he and Dad touched knuckles.

Colin started to climb onto the bus. Halfway up the steps, he turned to me. He pulled something out from under his Camp Snake Lake T-shirt.

It glittered in the sunlight.

The pendant!

Colin was wearing the pendant!

"Hey, Max—check out my new good-luck pendant!" he called, a big grin on his face.

"But that's *mine*!" I shouted.

"I'm tossing it to the snakes in Snake Lake! See ya!"

He disappeared into the bus, and it roared away.

A few minutes later, I sat on the edge of my bed, feeling glum. Nicky and Tara and I spent *months* searching for that pendant. And stupid Colin had it the whole time.

How could I tell my two ghost friends the bad news?

The house was silent. Mom and Dad had gone to a movie. I think they were seeing *Scream and Die 3*.

They both love totally violent movies with fighting and killing, and people thrown through plate glass windows, and guys screaming and dying hideous deaths every minute. Mom likes them even more than Dad. Go figure.

Well, I felt pretty violent myself. I wanted to *strangle* my brother Colin.

But he was gone. Gone for eight long weeks. And we *had* to get that pendant.

"Nicky? Tara? Where are you?" I called, glancing around my room.

No answer.

They had disappeared when Mom came bursting into my room.

"Hey, guys? Are you here? I need to tell you something."

No reply.

I climbed to my feet and started to pace back and forth. I had to calm down and stop feeling so angry. But how?

I called Aaron's house. His mother answered and said Aaron wasn't allowed to come to the phone. He was grounded because he'd played a joke on his little sister.

Aaron told his sister he had barfed in her bed. It was only potato salad. But when she saw the yellow pile on her blanket, she freaked and puked all over the floor.

"Aaron can come to the phone in about a month," his mom said.

I clicked off the phone and started pacing again. Then I picked up the deck of cards and shuffled it for a while. I practiced shuffling up and shuffling down. The trick is to keep the same five cards on top no matter how many times you shuffle the deck.

I'm getting pretty good at it. But shuffling cards didn't take my mind off Colin and the pendant.

"Nicky? Tara?" I called. "Where *are* you?"

The doorbell rang.

I jumped. I could hear my dog, Buster—our huge, furry wolfhound—barking his head off in the garage. Doorbells drive him crazy. I don't have a clue why.

The front door was open. I saw a man and a woman through the screen door. I blinked. Why did they look familiar?

The man was tall and thin and had wavy brown hair, thinning in front. He had serious brown eyes and a nice smile. He wore a white Polo shirt over baggy khakis.

The woman had lighter hair, cut short and straight. Her eyes were blue. They kept darting from side to side. She didn't smile. Instead, she was chewing the pink lipstick off her lips.

She wore a pale pink top over a flowered skirt with lots of pleats.

The man stared at me through the screen door. "I'm sorry to bother you," he said. "We're the Rolands. We used to live in your house. And we're searching for our two kids, Nicky and Tara."